SUPERNOVA

by
Russ Ebbets

© Copyright 1995

*for my athletes
past, present and future.*

Published by: Off The Road Press, P.O. Box 121, Seneca Falls, NY 13148-0121

All rights reserved.

No part of this book may be reproduced or transmitted in any form or by any means, electronic, mechanical, including photocopying, recording or by any storage system and retrieval system without written permission from the author, except for inclusion of brief quotations in critical articles or reviews. For information: Off The Road Press, P.O. Box 121, Seneca Falls, NY 13148-0121.

This book is a work of fiction. Names, characters, places, and incidents are either products of the author's imagination or are used fictitiously. Any resemblance to actual events or locales or persons, living or dead, is entirely coincidental.

Printed in the United States of America

Library of Congress Cataloguing-in-Publication Data

Ebbets, James Russell

Supernova
Russ Ebbets
ISBN 0-964827 9-0-5
1. Fiction. 2. Distance Running. 3. Sports

ACKNOWLEDGMENTS

Thanks to my teammates for the stories I needed.

Thanks to Anne Saslow for the patience I needed.

Thanks to Joe McDowell for the cover I needed.

Thank to Jan & John Ebbets for the encouragement I needed.

Thanks to Mike Blim for the truth I needed.

Thanks to Lori DeFurio for the typesetting I needed.

Thanks to Kevin Scheuer, Mike Reed, Mark Mindel and Timbo Orcutt for the details I needed.

Thanks to my father for Sunday afternoons,

And thanks to my mother for keeping it all together.

INVOCATION

The road is better than the inn.

— Cervantes

Far better it is to dare mighty things, than to take rank with those poor spirits who neither enjoy much nor suffer much. They live in the gray twilight that knows not victory nor defeat.

— Teddy Roosevelt

Biological evolution owes something to supernovas. Astronomers believe that supernovas are vital, that without supernovas, we wouldn't be here, life wouldn't exist on Earth.

As it is, with occasional imperfections, improvements come about and slowly life forms become more complex and better adapted to their surroundings.

— Isaac Asimov
Guide to Earth and Space

THE TRAIN

My father was a cripple.

He had gotten polio in World War II. He told me he felt sick one night and woke up paralyzed. He spend the rest of his life on one good leg.

He went to St. John's. He ran in a track meet there, once. He showed me a yellowed news article from the school paper. He won the 440. He ran 52 flat. He said he just ran it, he never trained. That was then.

When I was little, six or seven, he would take me to the train station every Sunday. About 3 p.m. a big freight train would pull out. The race would start with two toots of a horn, me and the train.

The rail bed was big blue stones. For 50, 60 or 70 yards I would pull away from the train. Then the tide would turn. Slowly the train would catch me. The engineer would smile and wave and disappear.

Breathless I would stagger back to my father, smiling. Today I had gone a little farther. He would smile back at me. I never beat the train, but I got the idea.

THE WORD

I arrived at freshman registration three hours early. The campus was empty. I parked my car at the Field House and walked to the track.

The track was black cinders, very black cinders. The curb was three inches high. I kicked it. There were white scuff marks on the curb. Not many, but some.

I bounced on my heels. There was no extra spring or give. High hurdle marks painted on the curb made me think. I stood at the start line and looked down the straight. What did Erv Hall see when he was in the starting blocks?

I began to walk the track and look at the stands, the trees, the Field House. Was Dave Patrick nervous every day as he prepared to anchor four relay teams at Penn? How intense were Liquori's workouts before he raced Jim Ryun?

I scanned the stadium. Where was Larry James when he realized he was better than Otis Hill? Was there anything in this stadium, this track that made Ron Delaney homesick?

I stood at the 3 mile start. Did Dick Beurkle's feet touch ground his first practice after his IC4A wins over Ron Stonitsch? Thoughts kept coming. What sense of opportunity did Morris

Morgan feel? Did the smile of Woo Woo Webster cover up the great weight of great expectations?

At what point in a later quarter did Tom Donnelly begin to persevere? Who felt the greater freedom from the classroom, Chris Mason or Greg Govan? I walked in wonder. No one was there. Was the air friend or foe to Don Bragg?

My solitary thought was shattered by the voice of a man, more leprechaun than man.

"You belong here?"

He wore a blue ball cap with a white V. His clothes ran together. The white trousers were dirty, the blue polo shirt pock marked by bleach. The shirt covered a belly the size of a basketball. The half bitten cigar in the side of his mouth made him look like a squirrel with a nut.

"You belong here?"

The question startled me. He was not a security guard. I was doing nothing wrong. I was only walking. His stare demanded an answer.

I began to mumble my name, that I was going to run track and asked if it was okay for me to walk on the track.

He looked me up and down. His stare was appraising. The moment was lengthened by his silence. He gave two chews to turn his cigar, took it from his mouth and spat.

"At Villanova you run," he put the cigar back in his mouth, "*run on the track.*" I stood corrected. I got the word. He turned and disappeared into the Field House.

PRETENDERS TO THE CROWN

Everybody came from somewhere.

A lot of guys came from Jersey, the Catholic League of New York, Long Island, Philly or somewhere next to nowhere in Pennsylvania. The real foreigners came from Ireland, Ohio, or some other distant spot that now had the distinction of sending someone to Villanova.

To these guys the Armory meant nothing. The Eastern States was a location; Van Cortlandt, a Dutch name. But to the man they could chase the white line and were only seconds away from their dreams.

There were a lot of names, Jake, Duke, Shep, Johnny Puma, Jackson, Steamin' Ian, Charlie Checkers, Frank, Tony the Parrot, Randy ROTC, Jay Brown, the Black Stone, Coach Frier, Mickey the Ratman, Wanda the Witch, Spot, the Rover Boys, Rhino Rothberg, The Wall, the Weasel and Eddie John Denny. I remember the names. Every name had a story. I remember the stories.

It was a time of great expectations. Reality ran a distant second to hope. There was no other way to live.

THE CHOSEN ONES

The Irish had it easy. By 18 or 19 they were already famous. They had it made. Their every move was chronicled in the press at home, detailed in periodic letters. Continued success would insure a lifetime of adulation and security. All they had to do was run.

By 14 or 15 you realize that much of life boils down to the road not taken; to chances and choices, made or missed.

We grow up in America told we could be President. Once upon a time it was an idyllic goal. The Irish had it different. From the time they could walk it was Ron Delaney.

Ireland is a third world country. You don't think of it that way, but it is. Beer may induce sentimental notions of the "Olde Sod" and people forget why they left. Long the bastard son of Britain, Ireland's recent past is little more than economic depression and internal strife. Ireland has long been a good place to be from.

Who could say if the pilgrimage to Villanova was a chance or a choice. But it was the opportunity he seized. Ron Delaney was a local hero who conquered the States and back home Villanova became a place where a man had a chance and a good man could be great.

Ron Delaney will be forever remembered for a day in Melbourne, a day when the sun set on the British Empire and the best runner in the world was not from England and not from Oxford. Ron Delaney proved to be an easy man to follow on the track, in the grand scheme, he was not.

But then what is success when the measure of a man is Ron Delaney? Villanova, Melbourne, the world record race at Sanby Stadium; their early success only narrowed the field. The Irish ran burdened with the weight of great expectations. The chance to dream gave no choice. Easy for the Irish was President.

THE LOCK

Ian cursed his lock and kicked his locker. Angrily he slapped the lock down. He had yet to perfect the combination sequence of right-left-right. He spun the dial again. The tug produced three quick curses; the lock would not comply and remained with secrets safe and guarded.

I asked if he needed help once, then twice. He answered on twice, "No...thanks," through clinched teeth. Again the lock slammed, frustration with intention. He was not going to get it.

I moved towards him. Ian was small for a runner, not one of Jumbo's leggy milers. He looked heavy too. There was no tone or tan to his skin. There was only a pasty white one could mistake for average.

"You start out with two full turns right to clear the tumblers." I reached for the lock. Ian blocked my help with his shoulder. I stepped back.

"You want some help or not?"

His hand held the lock tight. He didn't trust me for a second.

"Do you want to open it or not?" I didn't care. I was ready to run. He was not going to get it by himself. "Decide quick." The lock dragged from his hand and he stepped back. In a low voice he whispered, "14-24..." I turned to him and asked why he was whispering, no one was in the locker room. I spun the dial and saw Jake in the corner of my eye.

Ian said "42" as Jake stopped behind me.

"Whose locker is this?" there was a click.

Ian said it was his to which Jake shot back, "What is he doing?"

There was a silence. I concentrated on the lock. I spun the dial to 42, the lock opened with a click. Almost like an electric shock I felt a searing pain on my hamstring. I kicked my knee up smashing it into the locker door. I grabbed my hamstring. Jake clicked closed the red hot cap of his lighter and walked away.

Ian looked at me innocently. "Why does he do that?" He half turned dropping his pants to show me a red welt on the back of his leg. "He did that to me yesterday." He pulled his pants back up and turned to his open locker. Cigars, lighters, locks, there was a lot to learn.

"I would have got it, you know," there was no doubt.

"Sure," I thought, maybe in five or six years.

Quickly he dressed. We decided on the Tennis Courts. I moved towards the door and saw his hand move without hesitation. Click, click, the lock, then the locker were shut. He would be back. He turned and left with no doubt.

THE TABLE

You could talk at the table. The day began there and ended there and while you were there you talked track. Life was chronicled in miles run and quarters done. The language was cryptic at the table — the Frolic, the Big Hill, Radnor, the Tennis Courts, Mingus, Surekill, The Rose Garden, Jake. Other words — Van Cortlandt, the Armory, The Golden West, Easterns, IC's, Cemetery Hill, Manhattan. It all meant something. It meant everything, poetically.

Anyone could sit at the table, but why would they? The language was codified and cryptic — broomed, dropped, the boards, three lappers. To the unknowing it would be boring. To the unknowing Munich, Montreal and Moscow were just foreign places. For some it was the future. You were welcome to leave at any time. You dropped yourself.

The table was always within eyeshot of the ramp. You could see the limps and the smiles before you had to deal with the stories. We sat in muted paranoia, Sachel Paige be damned, we wanted to know who was coming. A good runner takes every advantage the course gives him.

What made the table was the people. Strong willed, good people, not afraid of work, pain or a struggle. Call it ego if you want — we all had goals and were only seconds away from our dreams. We knew this. Not many other 19 year olds could say that. Not many adults. It was all going to happen. We could feel it. We would prove it. The triumph of will.

The will was important. The weak ate alone. The personality was calloused by training and talk. Everyone came from somewhere and nobody's daddy had any pull at the end of the Frolic, at Surekill or on the boards. You were on your own. Self reliance made you strong.

The food was lousy at the table. It was always lousy. The Irish existed on toast and tea. What passed for hamburgers and hot dogs doubled as tactical weapons. There was little variation in the meals — eggs or cereal for breakfast, a lunch and supper. Our choices were austere.

The set-ups and get-backs were constant. There was no limit to good or bad taste. There could be none. It was a time of life when anything and everything must be a possibility. Time alone defined our limits and Time was to be defied.

There was a lot of talk at the table. Some guys never liked being second or third or whatever. The level of acceptance and complacency was low. The way up was over, around or through. You could be friendly, but...

Deference was deferred to greatness and greatness abounded. The best held sway and were allowed the final word. If you disagreed you got the chance to prove it on the track, the roads or the boards. Show up or shut up.

You learned things at the table. When the best guys talked you listened. The older guys knew the tricks. A second here, a second there — the seconds lead to firsts.

Conversations were dominated by wit, sarcasm and silence. Speed deferred respect. It might not be palatable but it was not arguable. The shared fatigue gave way to heightened emotions. People spoke their minds. There were no secrets. It was a time of free flow and laughter lifted the soul.

What one man designates as important another may see as insignificant. For the students their meals, their tables were a thrice daily ritual, attended and forgotten. At our tables we shared the center of the universe. And at the center was laughter. I remember the laughter.

BLINDED BY SCIENCE

Hyman Rickover is credited with being the father of the Nuclear Navy. The military superiority America enjoys on the sea is due almost solely to his vision and demanding expectations. The Vietnam War had all but eliminated the "military madness" of my generation but the Nuclear Navy was such an elite group it remained a worthwhile career goal for many.

We called him Randy ROTC — Cummings, Collins, Cunningham, I am not sure what his name was. It was always Randy ROTC to us.

The first time I met Randy ROTC was after lunch the second day of college. He stood outside Daugherty Hall at the center of a group of guys on the team. At 6'2", with a military haircut, a Chicago Cubs ball cap and the physique of Gumby, Randy was a comic figure.

I was about to ask someone who this guy was when Randy ROTC stopped mid-sentence and stared right at me.

"I don't know you!" he boomed and moved through the crowd towards me.

"I don't know you!" But the next thing I knew Randy had my hand in a vice grip and loudly announced he was, "Randy ROTC, Chicago, Illinois and I'm damn glad to meet you!"

In a state of complete self consciousness I mumbled my name, nodded my head and wondered why anyone would be so glad to meet me?

In the time that I came to know Randy ROTC I can say with certainty that he only ever met one man he was not "damn glad to meet." Do not get me wrong. In no way am I implying that Randy ROTC ran light in his loafers. Randy's father worked for Dale Carnegie and for his first 18 years he was weaned and preened on the power of a positive mental attitude.

Randy proved to be a wealth of maxims, morals and famous quotations that he was apt to quote, like a parrot, given the slightest provocation. At meal times one's only respite was to eat fast. If we were on a run salvation came by picking up the pace. I learned that, "The fool speaks his mind while the wise man listens." Randy could talk forever.

As an English major I had several required core sciences. The lab portion of the course was presented amphitheatre style with one instructor, his lab assistant Igor and 90-100 students. The instructors wore the clinical white coats. There were blue flamed Bunsen burners, rusting ring stands and beakers of bubbling water. A scientific ambiance pervaded the room.

To the snobs who were to become "real scientists" this lab was called "rocks for jocks." Personally I saw it more like Mr. Wizard. Nobody had any aspirations for a Nobel Prize — it was fun.

Nuclear Navy or not Randy ROTC sat next to me. "A good scientist must have a critical mind, always questioning," Randy had once enlightened me. Randy was enraptured with the experiments. As the mysteries of the chemical universe unfolded before us his fascination and wonder heightened. His questioning could be incessant. He left "no stone unturned" in his quest for scientific clarity.

And then came the day we made aspirin. The instructor and his assistant were going to synthesize common aspirin by combining ascetic acid and salicylic acid. The hypothesis was simple. There were only two materials necessary other than the usual apparatus. The procedure involved seven steps. Our results were perfect. Our conclusions flawless. It was that simple.

When the experiment ended the instructor presented the class with a little pile of white powder, not much larger than a quarter. He asked for questions. A scientist has a critical mind. A scientist leaves no stone unturned. Randy ROTC raised his hand, was acknowledged and rose to his feet.

"If that is truly aspirin," Randy challenged the professor, "how come it isn't in the shape of a pill?"

There was a great silence. I said to myself, "No." Not the short quick "no," but the kind where the "o" trails on for three of four seconds, a certain yes.

Why did we ever fear the Russians? Pogo was right, "I have seen the enemy, and it is us."

JAKE, VILLANOVA

Jake was an old fashioned trainer. He had spent a lifetime taping ankles, rubbing hot stuff on sore calves and spit on bruised egos. He always had a cigar in his mouth. A new cigar was half as big as Jake. Half as big.

The next time I saw Jake I still thought leprechaun. He was standing atop a nine foot ladder changing an eight foot light bulb. I had just gotten to my locker and was dressing hurriedly so as not to be late. Freshmen worry about these things. From the corner of my eye I studied Jake. There was a contrast of his height and shortness at the same time. He climbed down the ladder, folded it and proceeded to drag it down the hallway. The nine foot ladder and the four foot Jake. You only see things like this in the circus.

I guess I stared too long. When Jake got next to my locker he stopped. I tried not to notice him while intently noticing him. I turned to ask him if he needed help. He was chawing on his cigar to get it to his cheek so he could talk. There was an awkward silence. He looked up at me, "You belong here?" said the leprechaun. The older guys got a big kick out of this. Half dressed I did not know what to say. Jake turned and dragged the ladder away.

Jake was the king and court jester of the locker room. His office was an off white plaster room with a cracked mirror and cold metal benches. His locker room was a converted hallway.

Creature comforts included a concrete floor and clanging metal lockers. When it was crowded the only one who moved with ease was Jake. Without a word a path would open for his clear passage. You might think lighter, but it was because of the cigar.

Before nylon shorts you wore a jock. With years of practice Jake had perfected the ability to flick the ashes of his cigar with pinpoint accuracy. Jake would move through the crowded hallway, spot his victim, flick and move on. The ashes lay cradled in the jock pouch like a time bomb. Jake would be two or three steps away and then, HELLO! Some unlucky soul would be screaming and dancing and grabbing his groin. Jake innocently continued on his appointed rounds, mission accomplished.

Once you got to know Jake he would talk to you. You could say, "Jake, what's up?" and he would tell you the ceiling. Ask Jake what was new and he would say "New York." The guys from Jersey would say, "What about Jersey?" and Jake deadpan, "Can't say much about nothing," and walk off. Jake was never one to quibble over small points.

But you could not appreciate Jake until you saw the postcards. There were postcards all over the walls of his training room. There were new ones and old ones hung by Scotch tape and masking tape. There were notes from Dave Patrick from Europe, Marty Liquori from Mexico City and many cards from Ireland. The list of senders was impressive but what caught your attention was the address: Jake, Philadelphia, or Jake, Villanova University, USA — nothing more, an economy of language for an extraordinary man. You would watch him move and realize Jake was just as famous in the real world as he was in his own world. And you would also realize you were always watching that cigar.

STAIRWAY TO HEAVEN

I stood by my locker numbed by pain. I could not decide which leg to stand on. My feet felt like they had been beaten by a two by four. There was no way I was going to get my jock and shorts off without sitting down and there was no place to sit. At Villanova we run on the track and I figured, since no one else was doing it, we do not sit on the floor. I was having trouble with this.

Duke rounded the corner fresh from his shower. I was never formally introduced to him. I had only seen his heels for the first part of the Frolic before I got dropped.

"You ran OK today Russ, hang in there." He gave me a knowing nod and moved on.

How did he know my name? I was impressed. It made me feel good — at least inside.

I gripped the locker door with all my might. I can do this I thought. I bent forward like an old man and began to drop my shorts only to catch Jake making a path through the locker room. I rose with a creak and stared at Jake and his cigar.

Jake came to a stop at my locker.

"You runnin' yet?" he said with his cigar poking his cheek.

I told him I was trying to and he suggested, "You'll run faster with your shorts off your ankles."

A couple of guys started to laugh and Jake looked at them. That stopped that and Jake walked off.

I looked at the staircase, the big staircase that lead from the locker room. Supper was a long half mile past that staircase. I knew that whatever was going be served for supper would be great — if I could only get my jock off.

THE DROP LINE

Jay Brown and Duke used to talk about a guy named Banning, Bang Bang Banning. Everyday he ran the Frolic twice — ten miles in the AM, ten miles in the PM. At meals all Banning talked about was the guys he dropped. Bang Bang Banning dropped everybody, but he was a one season wonder. Bang Bang had fast times but no grades. Bang Bang got dropped by the Dean. Bang Bang Dean.

You learn early that you drop yourself. You ran and ran and ran and when you could not run anymore you dropped yourself. No one stopped to see what was the matter, how you were, they just ran on. The dead buried the dead. Like an old shoe or bad habit you were suddenly history. You could blame whoever you wanted but the truth was you dropped yourself. Bang, bang.

Everyday at practice you ran for the drop. Five or six guys would hit the road and after a mile things would get serious. Your hope was to catch a groove and avoid the grind; our death and taxes. It never got more complicated than putting one foot in front of the other but that could get to be the hardest thing to do. The second wind was always in your face.

It always seemed to be hang on. For a while you ran and then you tired. Was everybody tired? Was anybody? You wondered. Your eyes would dart left and right, you never looked or asked. Those were the signs you looked for, otherwise no one could know. You kept up the press. Your teammates kept up the pressure.

Somedays it was not worth it. You could drop back with the first to go, ease in from the Frolic or Tennis Courts. But some never gave up, never gave in. Ian would curse a bad day. He hung with speed and strength and when there was nothing left he hung by will, force of will.

How much could you will? Logic dictated a point. But what if there was none? Were you giving up? Were you weak? A quitter? He who lives to run away lives to run another day. You tried to convince yourself it was all mental and make another telephone pole or tree. It was will that made you step again.

Practice was a constant time of evaluation and introspection. Improvements came slower than calendar pages. Waiting for improvements could make time stand still. But we knew Time never did stand still. Impatiently we charged on, chasing the vanishing point.

You could sit at the table so dulled with fatigue you could not eat or if you had a bad workout you would not just to punish yourself — bed with no supper. No one would drive you harder than you would drive yourself. The other guys had their own agenda and you knew just as well as they did you were not part of it. In the back of your mind it was always find the crack, exploit the weakness, finish them before they finish you. Races are not won with second chances — only lost. Bang bang.

THREADS

Charlie in the Cage was as mean as a junk yard dog. When you stopped to think why there was little wonder. Imagine spending your life behind a metal fence where your only human interaction was with half naked guys trying to scam a towel off you.

Charlie in the Cage was older than dirt. He was skinny, with white hair and hated everybody. He would not give God the time of day, much less an extra towel.

Charlie was also in charge of sweats. The way he handed out sweats you would think he was giving away his own money. To every guy he said the same thing, "You lose 'em it's $75 bucks!" That was when 75 bucks was 75 bucks.

When I was in high school we were taught Bartleby the Scrivner. The teacher read, "Turkey felt his coat," with a great sense of satisfaction. He asked the class, "What do you think of that?" I already had figured out that Bartleby was a weirdo and was sure Turkey was not far behind. Like a horse feels his oats, Turkey felt his coat.

The first time I saw the Villanova sweats was in the IC4A Program. Billy McLaughlin had won some relay and there were three other guys holding the stick. Everyone was smiles. They looked pretty cool.

Throughout high school I had a picture of Pre chasing Donal Walsh off the flats at Van Cortlandt. Jumbo's singlet design was simple and clear. The runners made the statement.

Charlie in the Cage thumped my sweats on the counter, "That'll be $75 bucks if you lose 'em." I already knew that. I picked up my pile and moved to my locker. The sweats were heavy.

Piece by piece I hung the clothing in the locker. I had a few minutes so I decided to try on the fit. Everybody else was too. Guys were stretching out their arms and leaning over to see how long their cuffs were. Shep's comment about Ian's "high waters" lead Ian back to Charlie for a change.

Charlie's curse was loud and his "squat down" advice discouraged other clothing exchangers. Function would precede fashion just as statement would follow spectacle. Ian returned to his locker prepared for "the flood."

I walked into the bathroom only to catch Rhino Rothberg half flexing in the mirror and then trying to cover it up. Rhino stood a little taller and held his head a little higher. I looked at Rhino and said to myself, "Rhino felt his sweats."

"Nice threads, huh Rhino?"

Rhino self consciously looked down to brush a piece of lint off the blue satin jacket and answered with a simple, "Yes."

I put on my jacket and zipped the front and gave a little laugh to myself because if the truth be told — I felt my sweats too.

THE WALL

The Wall sat in a world of hurt. His nose and chin were bleeding. His front teeth were chipped. His pants were torn and his black wing tip shoes were scuffed to hell. He sat on his butt dazed and bleeding. His mechanical pens and pencils were scattered like pick-up sticks. For a moment spectators looked helplessly before they began to reflexively stomp the wind blown contents of his exploded briefcase.

The Wall suffered from EBS — Early Briefcase Syndrome. The Wall was a calculator boy who sported a bad haircut, brown high waters, white socks and black wing tips. His Foster Grants were Coke bottles. The Wall had more pocket pens than JC Penny.

The Wall was in my philosophy class. He knew who Martin Buber was. He knew who Maurice Morleau Ponty was too. When we studied Ponty's, "The Quasi-Corporeality of Signifying," the Wall understood. The Wall was the only one in class that talked, and he would talk. I would look out the window and think of practice.

The Wall had a favorite spot in the Pie Shoppe, a table near the wall. He would sit there with his buddy and discuss the theories, premises and postulates of the day. People left them alone. Even Hughie O'Kane.

The "Bricks" was roughly the center of campus with Dougherty Hall and the Pie Shoppe on one end and the mail room and student store at the other end. Before and after classes cliques would gather for a few minutes "at the Bricks." Everyone knew what that meant.

There were small grass plots surrounded by brick paths. The grass plots were also surrounded by a black plastic link fence. By design it was an uncomfortable seat. But it was a place to see and be seen.

The Wall was late. Conformity aside, using his geometric acumen he calculated that the shortest distance between two points was across the green patches. He began hopping the black plastic link fence and thumping across the green patches, hurdling chains and thumping again. He was not trying to sneak up on anyone.

We sat in our usual spot. The black plastic link fence was no higher than anywhere else. The Wall almost made the last stretch of black plastic chain link fence. He did catch his toe.

First the Wall emitted a grunt as his body went from vertical to horizontal. His glasses, briefcase and pens flew off him like pieces of a disintegrating missile. His arms reached for nothing but air. Gravity would not be denied. The Wall crashed, skidded and burned on the bricks.

Dazed and bleeding the Wall shifted to his butt as helpful hands and feet stomped and stamped the files and folders of his exploded briefcase, the genius work organized now is disarray. I looked at the Wall and thought of Buber and Ponty. There were red scuff marks on his white shirt and skid marks on the bricks from his hands. It did not quite fit but I remember thinking that there were bricks all over the Wall.

Shep had his hands in his pockets, he surveyed the destruction with a detached reality and pronounced to no one in particular, "I guess some people were never meant to run."

THE PIT OF YOUR STOMACH

Tuesday's lunch was never worth a damn. The rubber burgers and tube steaks were ignored. Tuesdays were speed days and it was only a matter of time before we would be on the track. The psyche-up had begun. Food was forgotten.

Class time after lunch time was wasted time. The afternoon was spent looking out the window. What was the weather? Was it hot? Was it cold? Was it windy? Would it rain? Your foot would get jumpy. The runs were coming. You were getting ready.

The workout would be quarters. It was always quarters. The quarters were not so bad, it was the jog. A two minute quarter on top of a 67, 68 or something faster. You recovered on the run, or at least you tried.

You could ease into the first five or six and try to catch a groove. The recovery was brisk, the pace was smooth. It all began pretty easy. As the light at the end of the tunnel began to fade the carrots appeared.

No man's land teetered between fitness and fatigue. The voices started. The count had begun. The "next one" came up quicker. How many were left? What number are we on? The line would begin to unravel. Guys cut corners on the jog to stay up. You forced yourself to hang. Silence answered the voices. There was no sympathy from the survivors. The dead buried the dead.

Fatigue changed the carrots from cheese steaks and milk shakes to ice cream or a beer. You could do an extra one for a beer. No one talked, a grunt sufficed. It got quiet, very quiet, save for the breathing. The breathing was deep and steady. Guys shook out their arms to get a grip.

The last carrot was water. The end was near. You could taste the water, dab it on your face, throw it in your eyes. The heart was pumping lactic acid and nothing would cut it like water. Get one more and get some water.

It took a minute or two after the end before you could breathe and jog, slowly. Packs of the dropped would form. The recovery was decided, an easy three — somewhere. Opinions were not strong. One's "hold on" was used up. We were ready for slow motions.

Later, at the supper table, Duke would sit in silence. He was a machine. Twelve, sixteen or twenty quarters knocked off like a shoulder shrug. If he was tired he never showed it. If he hurt he never said it. In between the table talk I noticed that. He lead us all, that must have given him something to think about.

PSYCHOLOGICAL WARFARE

Belmont Plateau, the cross country course at Fairmont Park in Philadelphia is the toughest cross country course in America. Van Cortlandt may have the name and Cemetery Hill more tradition but when it comes to difficulty Belmont gets the nod.

Van Cortlandt starts out flat, in fact the first mile has little more rise than level pavement. Belmont Plateau's first quarter is uphill, a pretty steep uphill, which everyone does in about 70 seconds. At the top you make a sharp switch back left around a tree. The next quarter is all down hill, a pretty steep downhill. Even if you are not running fast you can easily hit that quarter in 65. Figure this, you have just run a 2:15 half mile and you have a little less than five miles to go.

Belmont's exact distance was never known. It was dismissed as five miles but privately everyone felt it was closer to 5.2. The course was generally a minute slower than Van Cortlandt. Marty Liquori and Donal Walsh ran 25:12 the same year they were running in the low 24's at Van Cortlandt. There in lies the story that Jay Brown swore to me was true.

Fairmont Park is a long nine mile drive down Montgomery Avenue from campus. There was a red light every block and it could easily take 30 minutes or more if your timing was off.

Villanova's fall cross country schedule began with several easy dual meets, the Big Five Meet, the IC's and the NCAA's. The dual meets were against St. Joe's or Temple. We never lost. There never was much emphasis placed on these meets. They always seemed to be little more than a team time trial. The opponent usually had one good runner that cracked the top seven. The outcome was never in doubt.

Marty Liquori, by his senior year, was firmly established as one of the top distance runners in America, if not America's premier miler. His credentials were impressive. He was the last of three high school milers to break four minutes and made the Olympic team by beating Villanova great Dave Patrick. Liquori was an Olympic finalist at age 19 and the conqueror of Jim Ryun in two highly publicized duels.

Now imagine you are from St. Joe's or Temple or Penn and you are a good college distance runner. But this Saturday you are racing one of the best guys in the world. What do you tell your girl friend? What do you tell your friends? How do you feel going to the line?

This was not lost on Liquori. He figured that if his opponent was expecting a superhuman performance the worst he could do was let him down. So he decided to play a joke.

The day Liquori ran 25:12 at Belmont he almost missed the race. He got one of his buddies to drive down Montgomery Avenue and drop him off about three miles from the park. The friend was to drive to Belmont and tell a few people Marty was jogging in from campus, a nine mile warm-up.

It got to be race time — no Liquori. Both teams had their sweats off and were getting final race directions, no Liquori. The Villanova guys are not so concerned — we had a cast of thousands. The St. Joe's guys seemed disappointed. Jumbo is about ready to lose his mind and Coach Frier his job over — no Liquori.

And then, with a flair for the dramatic, from over the first hill jogs Liquori, blue sweats, gold letters, racing shoes in hand gliding down the hill with long graceful strides. All the while he had been jogging back and forth just out of view waiting, waiting for the correct time to make his entrance.

They held the race up for several minutes. Jumbo delivered some stern looks. Frier said some prayers. And not being in on the joke the team could not believe Liquori was going to run Belmont, the hardest cross country course there was, with a nine mile warm-up. But he did.

And he won and the time stands as one of the fastest times ever run on the course. His story done, Jay Brown would lean back his chair on two legs and state with great satisfaction, "It's the stuff of which legends are made."

DEFENDER OF THE FAITH

Sugar Ray Robinson once told Muhammad Ali that good fighters have bad hands and bad fighters have bad faces. Johnny Puma had a big nose. He came to Villanova to run but he was Canada's top Junior light heavyweight boxer. Johnny Puma's nose was straight as an arrow.

The first time I met Johnny Puma I liked him. He took me out to run The Big Hill. Ten minutes into an "easy" run I was breathing through a straw. Johnny chatted away. Johnny was the smartest guy on the team. I felt he knew everything. Racing, training, meals, girls, school, Jumbo, boxing — Johnny could cover a lot of ground in 30 minutes.

On the way we passed Valley Forge Military Academy. Johnny pointed out, "That's where your man Holden Caulfield went to school."

The "your man" was a necessary qualifier from the Canadian. Exactly who Holden Caulfield was I couldn't say. Not wanting to appear stupid — I didn't ask. I knew he never ran for Villanova. I never saw his name in Track and Field News. I figured he must have been a baseball player.

At the first party Johnny sat with several of us to have a beer. He said to no one in particular, "Alcohol kills your mitochondria."

I couldn't figure out if that was good or bad. Everyone laughed. I didn't know what a mitochondria was. Johnny Puma was not overly concerned. His cup was getting low. I poured him another beer; survival of the fittest.

Johnny spoke at length about several subjects and freely answered questions. It was easy to talk when you were not running flat out. The beer helped too.

Someone asked about initiations. Johnny got quiet, stared blankly into space for a second. "You don't have to worry about initiations...anymore," and he got up and left.

No one seemed to give "anymore" much thought, but it was clear Johnny did. "Anymore" hung in my head like an echo.

What the seniors knew about initiations they were not saying. Shep mentioned something about "no more six man lift." Jay Brown directed me to talk to Johnny Puma and laughed. Johnny would only shrug.

The man with the scoop was Ian. One day at the Pie Shoppe he told me everything. He leaned forward in his chair, "We don't have to worry about that...anymore." There was that "anymore" again. "Johnny P changed all that."

Ian said that when Johnny was a freshman the older guys had a trick called the "six man lift." At their first party, after a few beers, one of the seniors bet the freshmen that he could lift six of them at once. The other seniors volunteered, "He can do it!"

Johnny was picked as the middle man on the six man lift. Duke, Shep, Jay Brown and two other guys were laid all over Johnny. The senior grabbed Johnny's belt and grunted trying to lift all six guys at once.

What no one could see was the shaving cream the senior was unloading into Johnny's pants. Johnny never moved off the floor.

Johnny Puma stood up to jeering laughter. Suddenly in on the joke Johnny stepped forward and decked the guy with the shaving cream in one punch.

The next day Johnny Puma, with his big nose and cut knuckles, sat apart from the fat lips. The older guys never had much good to say about Johnny Puma after that, but at least they did have the good sense not to say it within his ear shot.

Two things were perfectly clear; Johnny Puma had come to Villanova to run and Sugar Ray Robinson was right.

DUNCAN KELLY

Man is made or unmade by himself, what we can do and what we chose to do is our choice. What I will always remember about Duke is the walk.

Johnny Puma said that Duke just appeared at the door of the Field House. Johnny was talking with Coach Frier on the sideline of the basketball court and Duke appeared in the doorway. The morning light shone gold on the floor. Duke walked right across the floor.

Duke carried an old army duffle bag that he gently rested on the floor. Johnny said he could see the initials DU.KE. marked with a blue pen drawn back and forth. DU.KE.

Coach Frier had spent most of the night at JFK International searching for Jumbo's lost recruit. To his disbelief and dismay he found that Duke's arrival time had been 8 a.m., not the 8 p.m. Jumbo had told him. Coach Frier was in a panic all night. Jumbo was never wrong and his top recruit was gone.

Johnny said the seniors did not let this go. He said the bleary eyed Frier sat at the table and two handed several cups of coffee in silence. The seniors were not silent. Every time a new face walked down the ramp or went for milk someone volunteered him as Frier's missing link. Frier took their hits like a wind blown paper bag. They only got worse.

And now before him stood a young man asking to be directed to Mr. Elliot's office. Duke raised his hand and introduced himself as Duncan Kelly from County Cork, Ireland. His accent was thick. Frier's hands were raised in prayer-like supplication. His eyes stared appraisingly at the unknown soldier. The phony brogue was not going to fool him. He could smell a set up when he saw one. He took his eyes off Duke and scanned the gym. There was no way he was going to fall for this. Uncharacteristically he snapped his welcome words to Duncan Kelly, "Prove it!"

Duke just stood there. His extended hand hung awkwardly unshaken and slowly lowered to his side. He began at the beginning.

The beginning was County Cork, Ireland. Two days before he had taken a bus to Dublin and yesterday he had taken a plane to America. The facts were clear with little elaboration and details. He waited four hours at the gate to meet Frier and he pulled a crumpled slip of paper from his pocket with a gate number, Frier's name and 8 a.m. to prove it. All this while Frier's eyes scanned the gym. He was not going to fall for this.

At noon he saw a priest and explained his situation. The priest paged Coach Frier. No one came. The priest called Villanova. No one knew anything about a Duncan Kelly.

On the back of Duke's crumpled slip of paper were directions from the priest from JFK to Penn Station and Philadelphia. The priest gave him $20 and good luck.

Duke caught the last train to Philly. He arrived downtown at 12:30 a.m.. It was late and dark and no one was around except the bums. Dragging all he owned he saw a cop. The cop was helpful but had bad news. Yes, he was at the right station, but the last train to Villanova had left 20 minutes before. There would be no more trains this night. The answer to Duke's next question was "about 14 miles."

Johnny said that when Duke said he decided to walk he scanned the gym too. Frier grunted, "Walk?" Duke said he walked 10 kilos everyday to school. He could not get lost if he followed the tracks. He shouldered his bag and walked.

Frier shook his head with little shakes. He raised his hand and signaled Duke to stop. Whoever had made this one up had won. "Okay, okay...Johnny take..." he paused, looking down to the faded green duffle bag, "...take Mr. Duke here to breakfast." And to breakfast they went.

Once on a warmdown, when we were alone I asked Duke about the walk. He shrugged it off, it never was a big deal to him. He laughed, "I was glad it wasn't raining," and then he told me about a teacher he had that had always told him, "Man is the maker and shaper of condition, desire and destiny," and in a very solemn tone said, "I always knew where I was going." As we jogged he stared at the ground and in a voice almost too faint to hear added, "...and when I don't, I have faith."

FATHER PAPIN

Father Papin was a man of many dimensions. He had studied in Rome. He had written books. He knew the Pope. He knew eight languages. And most importantly he knew what you knew — thought or spoken.

Father Papin arrived late to class that first Tuesday. Father Papin was hobbled with a bad back. He had a limp. He began attendance with a low voice. He was on the L's before the class quieted enough to respond. He finished attendance by saying, "If you did not hear your name called — you are absent. If you are absent twice — you fail." I thought that was a pretty stupid rule. Johnny DeFilise was a quick little guy from Brooklyn. He raised his hand to say he was here.

Johnny D was asked to stand. In clear and certain terms Father Papin repeated what he had said. Johnny D knew how to handle himself. He chewed gum. Johnny D was from a Catholic school in Brooklyn. Father Papin pointed to the door and told Johnny D from Brooklyn to go back to Brooklyn. Father Papin had our attention.

Father Papin then asked a question. "Who has read the Bible?" In a class of 40 only seven hands were raised. Father Papin dead panned, "I wanted to see who the Catholics are."

Several of us got the joke and laughed. I studied the man. There was a great energy about him — like a glowing jewel. I was exhilarated to study his manner. And then I realized his goal was sad commentary, not humor.

Father Papin taught Comparative Religion. We called it "The Grand Inquisition." Father Papin lead discussions on one's beliefs and actions. Introspection was required. Inspection was provided, by Father Papin. Father Papin strove to exhaust our knowledge on many subjects. For many the process was mercifully short, but even those souls developed an appreciation for eternity.

Our first essay exam had only one question, "How have I matured since I entered college?" The pages of our blue books got very white and for some of us they stayed that way.

Father Papin was always late to class. To his credit, to our fear he always arrived. One day he was 25 minutes late. Everyone had left save six of us. Individually he asked each of us why we waited. When it was my turn I simply told him, "You are always late, I knew you'd come." He stared at me in silence. He stared through to my soul, I am sure of it. It was an odd feeling. He never said a word. I thought, "The truth will set you free." I felt that, but I did not know that, yet.

High comedy with slow torture marked the classes after a Papin test. Alphabetically he would humiliate the roster. Your name was called. You rose and were asked to grade yourself. The smart people at the top of the alphabet confidently deserved an A or B+. "Do you think that someone who cannot spell 'catechism' deserves an A?"

"Your thought" soon lead from a B+, to a B, C+, C, a begging C. "I studied hard," was the common plea. Father Papin would listen a few seconds longer only to raise his hand. There was silence. The student was told to sit. The next name was called.

My name was called. Slowly I rose. I had a plan. I had decided to ask for a C+, suffer a few barbs and settle for the hook. It was foolproof.

Father Papin raised his eyes from my bluebook, "Who wrote the Consul of Philosophy?"

For the longest second I stood there. I could not remember what I had eaten for breakfast and he wanted the answer to a question from a week ago? I felt foolish. There were no whispered hints, no one in the class knew. I vaguely remembered something about Diadaké. I went with Diadaké.

"Diadaké was the author of the Consul of Philosophy." I spoke with confidence.

He raised his eyes. I could feel him looking at my soul again. He was looking for the truth. I began to repeat my answer when he gave two small grunts, something that passed for a laugh.

Evidently I had said something wrong, although I had no idea what it was. I knew Diadaké was an answer on the test.

"If one of my graduate students gave such a foolish answer I would have him dismissed from the program."

Oh-oh — that did not have a good sound. I had a "Back to Brooklyn" feeling in the pit of my stomach. I knew Diadaké had something to do with the test. It probably was not associated with the Consul of Philosophy.

"You have the correct answer on your paper — why don't you know the answer now?" His words were spoken with a rhetorical slowness. I did not like where this was going.

"Forgetting" is always a lame excuse. My plan was crumbling. With great hesitation I announced, "I guess I forgot."

Father Papin's eyes had drifted back to my blue book. I think he mumbled, "He's not sure if he forgot." My ship was sinking. I was called to the front of the class.

This was not good. He had never done this before. This was not good. Standing at his desk I looked at my blue book. Then our eyes met, "You cheated," he said.

There were no appeals to a Papin Verdict. I was dead in the water. This was a moment of clarity I shall never forget. Icy balls, literally balls of sweat ran down my flanks. I was terrified. I began to mumble my defense only to be cut off with...

"You cheated."

In shock the silence was deafening. The gladiator moved for the kill. The class sat in silent transfiction. Once more I tried to explain.

"You cheated," slapped me back to reality.

I was angry and ashamed. Father Papin had come late to class that test day. Someone had noticed that behind the drawn maps of the Holy Land were the ten questions of our mid-term.

Up went the maps. Frantically I and the whole class paged through our textbooks to verify our answers. Father Papin was sighted. Down came the maps. I never touched the maps. I did look at the board but I never touched the maps. Damn! Resistance was useless. Ashamedly I dropped my head and almost to myself mumbled, "Yes."

"What will your parents say when you are expelled from school? What will you do?" Here I am twisting in the wind and Father Papin begins to jab me with the Catholic guilt stick.

I had no idea. I had no ideas left. There were several more unanswerable questions. Father Papin made a comment that caused the class to burst into laughter. He let it go for a second then slammed his hand to the desk. There was an immediate silence. The verdict was reached.

Father Papin scanned the class. In his slow and careful manner he began, "Before you stands a cheater. You know this and so do I. But the difference between this person and you," he paused an instant to look into *their* souls, "is that he is the only one with the guts," guts was drawn out like a sizzling brand mark, "the only one with the guts to admit he was a cheater. You are all cheaters."

You are all cheaters — it didn't make me feel good, but it did make me feel better. Although my immediate future was unclear "guts" was something to build on. It was the happiest 'C' I ever got.

THE RATMAN COMETH

With 125 yards to go in the IC4A JV Cross Country Race Mickey Delaney had no idea how far he had to go. He had already "kicked" twice hoping the finish line was around the next bend. To a Massachusetts native Van Cortlandt Park offered no familiar landmarks. The finish stretch was an endless black cinder trail one inch short of infinity.

The cheers of the crowd were deafening. Mickey's thought was frenzy. Ahead teammate Keith McClancey faltered as Penn's Bobby Morman moved for the lead. Mustering his last ounce of resolve Mickey kicked again.

Early that morning Mickey had announced to all that he was "mad" and that today he would show "no mercy." With 50 yards to go there was only Morman between Mickey and the finish line. In spite of the running prowess of a Dave Merrick or a Dennis Fikes Penn's runners were not held in high esteem. A loss to a "girl" would make for a long ride home. There would be some dignity in dying trying. The finish line appeared. Mickey won by a step.

There was no one more surprised by the victory than Mickey himself. Experimenting with a "new breakfast" that morning had left him car sick on the way up. Within the first mile he developed a cramp and faded to 50th place in the Van Cortlandt hills. The DNF weighed heavily on his mind, but then he stumbled, all but fell to the ground and regaining his balance suddenly felt better. Systematically he began to chew up his competition, true to his word, with no mercy.

At the base of Cemetery Hill Mickey ran a strong 10th. Ahead Keith lead a small pack of runners. For many Cemetery Hill is an unpleasant memory of Van Cortlandt. By the top Mickey was in 5th place. It was the last thing Mickey said he clearly remembered.

The coaches gathered at the second floor of the Terminal Bar to score the race and drink beer. The athletes gathered downstairs. Collegiate alliances temporarily melted. It was a chance to see old buddies and talk of old times, the past season and indoor hopes. The pressure was off for everyone except Mickey.

In spite of his victory Mickey sat subdued and distracted at the Terminal Bar. As a pre-med major today's race had forced Mickey to miss a lab practical test. The professor had gone out of his way to imply that were Mickey to miss the test there would be little chance of him succeeding in medicine. It was a great deal of guilt to heap on a freshman. Mickey decided to run.

In an effort to make Mickey's decision as distasteful as possible the professor scheduled Mickey's test that evening after he returned from the race. A proctor was assigned and Mickey was to anesthetize a rat and dissect the animal as per the directions of the proctor. As we sat in the Terminal Bar Mickey sat cold and alone with his books in the back of the van studying the guts of a rat.

Back at Villanova the school day ended and Mickey's professor left for home. The professor forgot to leave a rat for Mickey's test. When Mickey met the proctor at 7:30 there was no rat to be found. Mickey had been warned that there would be no excuses, no explanations accepted. With the proctor he searched every cupboard, every possible hiding place, no rat.

The proctor had a ring of keys and began to search in other rooms. The second room produced a rat. With a sigh of relief, a prayer for forgiveness and no mercy Mickey sacrificed the rat. Meticulously the dissection was performed. By 10:30 that night, with the aid of several beers, Mickey was on his feet.

"I showed Cemetery Hill no mercy!" he thrust his arm into the air. "I showed Bobby Morman no mercy!" again he thrust his arm into the air. "And I showed that rat no mercy!" Mickey's arm raised his beer roughly in the direction of his mouth. Mickey had the kind of day that teases an 18 year old with thoughts of immortality.

By lunch the next day Mickey was mired neck deep in reality. We all thought "hangover" when we saw Mickey distractedly trudge down the ramp. His meal tray clanged on the table. He plopped into his seat. Our diagnosis was immediately upgraded to "bad hangover."

"I killed Disney's rat." he mumbled to no one in particular. "I killed Disney's rat and I might get thrown out of school." No one had the slightest idea what he was talking about. To our fascinated disbelief he explained. In no time we were giddily repeating to ourselves, "Mickey killed Disney's rat!"

Disney's rat was the sole survivor of over 400 test rats that had been subjected to astronomically high radiation levels. The government had given Villanova thousands and thousands of dollars for this experiment. Dr. Disney, a distant relation of Walt, had worked years on this experiment. Mickey killed Disney's rat, Mickey killed the wrong rat! It was unbelievable.

Johnny Puma arrived to the table late. He sat quietly at the end of the table and ate his lunch while Mickey finished his story. As a senior biology major Johnny already knew the news. He also knew how Mickey felt about mercy and that the biology professor was in more trouble than Mickey was. In fact Mickey was not even to be reprimanded. But this was an opportunity not to be missed. Breaking a momentary silence Johnny dead panned, "So Ratmen, now that you have a rat under your belt, who is next...Mickey Mouse?" That had guys gagging on their food and milk shooting through noses.

What goes around, comes around. The rat gave us a handle on Mickey we never let him forget. He was contacted via the "rat line." His friends were referred to as the "rat pack." At social functions he was on a "rat patrol." From that moment on and forever after "The Ratman Cometh," and true to his word Mickey was shown no mercy.

THE BEAUTY OF THE ROSE

I never liked Charlie Checkers. It probably had something to do with Charlie's "Which way to the country club?" attitude that he accentuated with pink Izod polo shirts, lemon yellow slacks and a pair of green plaid pants he wore like a tattoo. The fact that Charlie represented the next rung on my personal ladder to fame had nothing to do with it.

So the fact that Charlie had run afoul of Shep generated little sympathy from me. Shep had a way of putting someone in his place in a hurry. As freshmen we were slow moving targets for Shep.

Charlie made it a Friday habit to forecast each weekend's romantic adventure. He envisioned himself as an unconscious lover that every coed on the Main Line dreamed of. Speaking from this pretext he began his monologue only to be cut off mid-sentence by Shep.

"Charlie," Shep spoke with authority, "You couldn't get laid with a blank check or a fist full of twenties."

That sank Charlie's Friday love boat forever, amen.

As for myself, I had Lauren. I did not really have her, but I figured it was just a matter of time. Lauren was the most beautiful girl I had ever seen. The first time I saw her she stood like an armed Venus in the Freshman Registration line. She stood alone and aloof, apart from the nervousness and chatter. She had a style and grace beyond her 18 years.

The problem was how could I get close enough to tell her that. None of my friends knew her friends. She seemed enamored by the seniors. I was not deterred. Something good was going to happen. I had that feeling.

Then I had the Father Papin debacle. I became a bit of a legend. I did not brag about it. Part of my Papin rehabilitation was to work in his research group. He hand picked the top five or six students from each class, and me, to do research articles for him. Penance, I guess.

Father Papin had two classes. In the "research group" from the other class was Lauren. The groups met on a regular basis. I devised a plan. I would walk Lauren home, talk about Father Papin and ask her out. Heaven loomed around the corner.

There were many walks, and long talks and things progressed with Lauren. A movie, a milkshake, a peck on the cheek. I had hope, and he that has hope has everything.

Thanksgiving vacation was coming. Lauren lived in North Jersey. It was on the way home. I offered her a ride. She accepted. The ride would take two and a half hours. Two and a half hours with Lauren! I was in heaven. Heaven!

This was my big chance, my breakthrough. I saw a movie where the leading man gave his sweetheart a rose. It was very romantic. It worked for him. A rose, I could do that.

I located a florist in Ardmore. It was the afternoon we were to leave. I got the rose. Walking back to the car I wondered where to put the rose. The rose could not go back to the dorm. I would only be caught dead with flowers. Someone called my name. It was Frank...and I was dead.

I felt terror in my heart. If word ever got back to the table I had bought a rose for Lauren — it would not be good. For three panic stricken seconds I stood speechless.

"A present for your mother?" Frank volunteered.

"One is all I could afford." I tried to laugh.

"Charlie got his mother some flowers too." He added that it was a nice idea and that maybe he should get something for his mother. I knew that there would be no "rose talk" at the table, mothers were okay. I put the rose in the trunk.

The little note card was still a problem. All week long I had read Shelley, Keats, Shakespeare — nothing was right. My list of notes was long and jumbled. Everything seemed insincere and contrived. How could I compare Lauren to a rose?

And then by chance, by some miraculous chance I transposed the idea. I compared Lauren to the rose. It had everything I wanted. There was flow. There was flattery. It could not fail to touch her. I confidently wrote, "The beauty of the rose pales when compared to you." Success!

I arrived early at the Good Council Dorm armed with my rose. I strode to the desk and had Lauren paged. They were supreme moments of anticipation. Most certainly another breakthrough. I gently placed the rose on the shoulder of the sofa, sat, and fixed my gaze on the cathedral doors from which Lauren would ascend.

My reverie was disrupted when who should walk into the lobby but Charlie Checkers in a blue blazer and his green plaid pants. In his hand was a bouquet of daisies and some other pink flowers. Mother my foot! Blank Check Charlie had a woman!

Charlie did not see me for a moment. He fidgeted with his jacket and straightened his tie from some circle jerk fraternity. I tried to envision his princess. No doubt some 9 o'clock Catholic girl who did not drink, know sports or know Charlie. I had Charlie pegged.

And the cathedral doors opened. It was Lauren. She wore a white blouse. The sight of her made my heart flutter. I rose with my rose to meet her. She did not see me. She stepped towards Charlie.

Lauren smiled, spread her arms and planted a big kiss right on Charlie Checkers's lips. Slowly, like a deflated balloon, I sank to the sofa. I looked at my simple rose. The beauty of the rose looked pretty pale to me. I put the rose on the back of the sofa and eased it to the floor. You win some, you lose some, and some you never forget.

SPOT REMOVER

My favorite dog story is James Thurber's, *Snapshot of a Dog*, the story of an AMERICAN bull terrier. The first time I read the story it put a lump in my throat. While Lassie and Thurber's Rex may represent one side of the canine spectrum there is a dark side too, the leg biters and runner chasers. It seems inevitable if you run long enough you meet up with one of those twisted souls. There is a set of teeth out there with your name on them.

Spot was a Dalmatian, but Spot was not his real name. No one ever took the time to find out. No one cared to. Spot's territory was located half a mile from the end of the Tennis Court loop, an eight mile circuit of upper middle class suburbia, palatial estates and private tennis courts.

The Tennis Courts ran through two women's colleges, the exclusive Bryn Mawr ("only our failures marry") and the common Harcum Junior College (Harkum, parkum and etc.). The coeds offered a fleeting respite from the fatigue of the road and spurred conversation until we crested the final hill.

It was not a hill of any note, maybe 50 yards downhill and 150 yards of flat, The Valley of Spot. The silence of the run was always broken by a muttered wish that Spot be tied up that day. Someone else would lament they did not feel like sprinting. And finally, without fail, someone would mention Rhino Rothberg and chuckle.

All the while this chummy talk disguised the cold calculations we made as to who we could out kick. Spot was a clever, wise hunter. He would not foolishly chase the fast twitchers with the 49 point speed. He wanted the aerobic boys that red lined out at a 55 second quarter.

Moving downhill the pace would quicken. We used the hill to jumpstart our sprint. We ran defensively, alert and aware for that muffled growl and that low kamikaze attack. Some days nothing happened. Other days you ran for your life.

If the truth be known only one runner ever got bit. Rhino Rothberg was hobbling home in the breakdown lane with a bum Achilles when it happened. In fact, to hear Rhino tell the tale you would wonder how he got teeth marks in his hamstring. The only thing Rhino remembered was standing on the hood of some guy's car, blood oozing out his leg and a snarling dog baiting him to come down.

I could only imagine what Spot was in a previous life. It was God's cruel joke on Spot to parade all that lean meat by him daily, almost there, but never there. Spot was a canine Sisyphus. Spot only had three legs.

Three legs or not Spot always got our attention and had our respect. As far as we were concerned he had one notch on his gun and nobody was volunteering to be the second. Rhino missed three weeks training. Fear is a great motivator. On cue we would dig down and never look back.

Jay Brown was a native New Englander, compactly built with a quiet pride that only improved his ability. Never in the lime light his career was a side light, he was a journeyman Yankee for the team. But Jay left behind a legacy that will never be forgotten.

Jay always ran the Tennis Courts on Tuesdays as his morning warm-up for the afternoon speed workout. At lunch, we would all gather at the table at the bottom of a glass enclosed ramp to eat and get psyched for that afternoon.

Jay came down the ramp that Tuesday and uncharacteristically banged the glass enclosure. Gaining our attention we saw a smile from ear to ear. He cocked back his head and punched his fist into the air. Something was up.

In the 30 seconds Jay disappeared to get his lunch speculation settled on the fact that he must have been admitted to law school. Still smiling, Jay strode triumphant to the table, dropped his tray, spread his arms out wide and proudly announced, "Call me the Spot Remover!"

Holding court Jay detailed how he felt sluggish throughout his run and that as he crested the hill to The Valley Of Spot he resolved only to go as fast as needed. Spot lived on the left side of the road. Jay chose the right side, hoping to avoid a chase.

"Fortunately," he paused for a second, "I was out of luck."

Spot tipped his hand early with a bark to which Jay shifted gears. There was a line of cars on the left side of the road and while Jay could not see Spot he could hear the barks. Finding an opening, Spot focused on Jay and made his final mistake.

It seems there was a 70 year old lady driving a Fleetwood Cadillac "10 knuckles and a nose" towards Jay. Whether she saw Jay or not he never said. A devilish grin crept onto his face as he pronounced that, "Poor Spot never..." and the rest was drowned out by our cheers.

One by one we ceremoniously rose to shake Jay's hand and when it was Rhino's turn he gave Jay a big bear hug.

THE CURVE

Mickey Delaney was fit to be tied. When he banged his fork on his tray and the table shook. Little bits of food were flying everywhere. The last two words of every sentence ended with "mother fucker."

Purple veins bulged in his neck. Every time he spoke little bits of food sprayed randomly. A chunk of something landed on Rhino Rothberg's plate. Rhino pushed it aside with the end of his fork. No one was laughing.

Charlie Checkers was cool, but he never took his eyes off Mickey. "What are you so beefed about? You passed!"

It was the wrong thing to say. Gas on fire. I thought Mickey was going to start throwing things, I kept my eye on his knife. The curses continued. But really, how could Charlie have known? Nobody knew.

Mickey had walked out of his first accounting test confident, "I rocked it!" he told Charlie, Ian and Jack Rash. "It's easy," and then he proceeded to tell them all the questions and answers. Mickey had a good memory. The B section, Charlie's section, had the same test.

Mickey got 90% of his answers right. Mickey was very smart. If you had doubts you could ask him. The problem was that the average grade for Mickey's section and Charlie's section was 90. Overall Mickey was "average," and Mickey was never "average." In fact Mickey had gotten the third highest mark in his section. Mickey got a "C."

Ian got a hook too, but what steamed Mickey was that Charlie had gotten an "A."

I just thought "college can be rough," but I said nothing. I was not about to offer advice or consolation after my Father Papin incident. I was still licking my wounds.

Shep sat amused at the freshman growing pains. "Well," he said, "I hope you learned something." Mickey quieted enough to take a breath. His hands rested on his tray. Everyone hung on Shep's words of wisdom.

"The moral of this story is..."

But before he could finish Randy ROTC, caught up in his own evangelical zeal blurted, "Cheaters never prosper!"

I could see Mickey swallow a lump of food whole. Randy had just added his name to Mickey's list.

Shep shook his head and gave a sour look at the disturbance, "No you dummy," he said to Randy as he turned to Mickey, "The moral of the story is — never take the first section!" And then Shep reared back his head and laughed.

THE BOARDS

They kept the wood track stacked under the football stadium seven months of the year. Once football ended they would start to assemble the track. It would take two days. As the guys on the team came down the ramp they would announce, "The boards are going up!" like no one else knew. The season was changing. You could feel it in the pit of your stomach.

It was all business on the boards. It was never warm. The days were gray and a wind could make an hour last forever. Nothing was ever funny on the boards. There was a job to do that was not going to be easy. You might not be successful and it was going to hurt more than a little. There was not much to smile about on the boards.

Cross country was finishing up and at the end of the Frolic or Tennis Courts you would jog over and take a few laps on the boards just to feel. The quarter milers and "lazy" 800 guys would be there, their workouts begun in earnest. By suppertime everyone knew what the workouts were on the boards. There was a certain anxiety, no one worried if it was too much too soon. It was always — could I do that?

It was cold on the boards. They were outside and when they set up the track east of the football stadium there was much cursing by the older guys. The sun would set behind the stadium around 3:30. Most people never appreciate the winter sun. No one does until you lose it.

The cold tempered the will. The cold developed a certain resiliency. You became strong from the running and strong from the cold. You had no choice.

We ran in blue racing tights. They were a thick navy cotton blend with knee pads. Most of us cut the knee pads off. Being called a "knee pad boy" was an insult you only suffered once. Anyway, knee pads restricted your motion.

We trained running inside left, we recovered jogging inside right in the outside lane. The bank was the steepest there and as fatigue set in legs could get wobbly. Unintentional bumping drew stern looks and curt commands, "Suck it up!" or "Pay attention!" You forced yourself to recover and strained to keep your focus as your body ground to a halt polluted with lactic acid. An hour on the boards could be hell.

We ran in single file — on the train. No one tried to pass. You just held on in groups of three to seven, no spurts, no tactics, just smooth running. The leaders changed each interval. Someone new to cut the wind, set the pace. You could tuck in and "rest" at 60 second pace. We started off on the run and never stopped.

Jumbo never missed a workout. He stood in a little green box like a phone booth. He always wore a dark overcoat, a hat and goulashes. As you ran by you could see the stopwatch in his hand. He would call out one or two times. If you were at the end of the line you had to figure it out. We ran, he talked. It was about the only time he ever talked.

Repairs on the boards stuck out like sore thumbs. The new wood was a virgin white pine. Everyone would get their spikes on and go to the new wood and step on it, leave their mark, break in the new wood. It was good luck.

I used to look at all the spike marks on the boards. There must have been a million. All the wood was splintered and stamped down. In moments of existential clarity I used to wonder about the spike marks. Some were made by Liquori, Patrick, Delaney, Irv Hall, Larry James — who knew who made which mark. It made you wonder. Fatigue is an odd thing. The recovery ended and we were off again.

THE SECRET

Free, white and 18 can give license to cynicism. George Stone was none. When the Irish guys called him the Black Stone, George would just smile. To the white guys he was just George, an oddity, a black distance runner.

George was from South Philly. It was an area more prone to produce a boxer or a basketball player or junkie than a runner. It never seemed to bother George. It did not seem to matter so much where you came from as where you were going; like a race.

You had to ask George questions to get him to talk. He was from a gang, the Omegas, and had a brand mark on his arm to prove it. When I asked him what it stood for he said, "Omega," like I was supposed to know what that meant.

George was meticulous in his every action. His locker was spotless, never cluttered. Going to class he walked fast, by himself. He never carried many books, just what he needed. Most of the time he trained alone. It was his choice.

Once on a run I asked him how he got started running. He told me his ninth birthday was a picnic party at Fairmont Park and he saw men racing. He ran to the finish to see Oscar Moore win the race.

As Oscar Moore walked after the race George followed finally summoning up enough courage to approach the man. George told me he asked Oscar Moore what was his secret, what would he have to do to run like him.

Oscar Moore smiled and said, "Read a book a week, read biographies, they give you examples...and always be a gentleman."

I thought for a few seconds before I replied, "George, everybody says that...nobody listens to that stuff...you hear it all the time...it never makes any difference."

George was silent for a long second before he volunteered, "It did to me."

FRESHMAN FEAR

The freshmen at Villanova are in a unique situation. To the man they have some story to tell of how they won a big race. And if they lost the big race there was a good chance their conqueror was sitting next to them at the table. It was understood that if you top out on this team there would not be much concern for the competition because you had already beaten them. An even if you did not you were already traveling in company daddy's money could not buy.

There was a distinct pecking order on the team. Everyone knew who could "drop" who. It was not anything one bragged about, it was just known. On the other hand it presented a goal, something or someone to shoot for. The ladder to success was your teammates. You dropped them one at a time. Ultimately there would be one survivor. The dead buried the dead.

But it never got morose. There was exhilaration each day at practice. We knew we were going to run fast, and running fast was what life was about.

Interval training on the boards was not fun. Everyone knew the track could drop them. It seemed to be survival from the start, a single file line of three to seven runners. We ran three lappers, some 465 yards in 63 seconds. The recovery was "brisk." We ran the recovery jog in reverse. Stop, turn, repeat. The best could easily do ten three lappers. The rest would fade along the way, dropped, the victims of a bad day or poor genes.

Jumbo only talked to three or four of the older runners. They would rejoin the group as we did our strides and "the word" would spread. On the boards it was always two or three lappers.

Jack Shepard was the defending NCAA 1000 yard champion. He had been a 1:52 880 man for one of the Catholic high schools in "the city" — New York City. He was particular how you pronounced the name of his high school. His high school teammate went to Manhattan College. Shep loved to beat him. Shep would get loud, "He can take me out and I run him down, and if he lets me sit...I outkick him!" Shep loved to laugh.

The NCAA indoor meet was held in Detroit's Cobo Arena. It was a four lane, eleven lap track, an intimate racing surface. When Shep won the 1000 no one expected it. He never said he did. But he did like to show you the diamond in the ring that had NCAA champion etched on the side.

Marcel LaRue from Fordham had dominated the indoor circuit; Millrose, the IC4A's and had met his match in King Congo from Southern Illinois. They had effectively broken the field with Shep racing a clear third. No one knows who spoke first or who swung second but in an instant Congo and LaRue squared off on the track. Shep saw an opening, used a little subway shove and a lap later Jumbo had another NCAA champion. Shep laughed on.

But Shep never laughed on the boards, and he had a lot of trouble with freshmen. The trouble with freshmen was they did not know what to do. After years of training alone, always pushing the point they were now forced to share the track with others. It took practice to get into the flow.

We all knew that with time, work and patience the track might someday be ours. But you do not get your dreams until you pay your dues. It took awhile until you turned in the right direction, until you knew what to do and until you could keep up. And then the new frosh would arrive to mess up the rhythm.

Shep used to wear red Puma spikes for speedwork. They were red velvet with a white spot on the heel. Inside the white spot was a little black leaping puma. On the recovery jogs you made a study of your teammates shoes and legs. By the fifth three lapper that is all you cared to see. You forced yourself to recover as you held on. You were there for a reason. You hurt for a purpose. It was a concentrated environment.

But one recovery jog is forever etched in my mind. I was following Shep, exhaling hard, straining to gather myself. I spit. Generally I considered myself a good spitter. Fatigue, I found, not only deadens the senses but affects the aim. A soft, white spittle, that started out with the good intentions, got caught in the air and landed on Shep's heel. Ordinarily such a chance shot would get a big laugh. But we were on the boards. Nothing was funny on the boards.

Here I was a lost freshman, hardly done a thing right since I started running and now I had spit on Shep, the NCAA champion. White on red. I was sure everyone saw it. I was sure everyone was saying, "He spit on Shep, the NCAA champ!"

I ran the next interval fast, on fear alone. I could not believe what I had done. The spittle hung tenaciously to Shep's heel. I reached my limit on the next interval. There was no way to hide the evidence. I warmed down quickly and got out of the locker room before the best guys got in.

That night at the table everyone agreed it had been a good workout. Shep looked around the table and said, "Somebody spit on my shoe today." There was a long silence. "It was probably one of you freshmen." We all looked at each other dumbly.

Duke said, "Oh Shep...you probably spit on yourself!" There was a burst of laughter and general agreement at the table. Duke could do that. He ran a 3:54 mile. And then Duke stared right at me.

EDDIE JOHN DENNY

Rhino Rothberg never spoke. He was a Jew among Gentiles but that had nothing to do with it. Rhino was a man of action, not words. He could sit a whole week at the end of the table and never utter a word. Rhino just ran. He was the Jersey, Eastern States and Golden West Champ. He never lost in his last two years in high school. He took Bill Dabney of Boys High to the line more than once. Nobody else could say that. Rhino, just didn't.

"You are Eddie John Denny," said Rhino, with what was almost a double take.

Our heads did double take. Rhino had spoken. Who was Eddie John Denny? Before us stood a guy of medium build, height and weight, tray in hand. He took an open spot at the table, placed his tray and raised a fist to his forehead. He extended his index finger, "Save the Rhinos!" were Eddie John Denny's first words. Rhino smiled.

He was Eddie John Denny. Eddie John Denny introduced himself with three names. He spoke fast and his hands moved quickly. He had just transferred from Manhattan and was he glad to be here! He said he was tired of running Keogh, Colon and Savage into the ground. He got a good laugh out of this. So did Rhino. We sat in silence. Our eyes met but we made no connections. Who was this guy?

Eddie John Denny did come from Manhattan. He had run there but he was more a man of words than action. Rhino knew Eddie John Denny from the Armory. Everybody from the Armory knew Eddie John Denny. Eddie John Denny could always be found down in the hallway running a dice game or dealing ten guys blackjack. Eddie John Denny had a reputation.

During his senior year Eddie John Denny showed up at the Loughlin Games Frosh-Soph Meet dressed in white coveralls with "Maintenance" stitched over the left breast. He set up post outside the men's room. He got there early and encouraged everyone to stop by often.

Eddie John Denny had rolls of toilet paper, a few bars of motel soap and some clean towels. It was just like the race track. For a small "donation" you could have all the comforts of home. Business was brisk. The customers were happy.

By noon Eddie John Denny had a wad of bills like a guy running a gas station, which in a way, he was. Things would have gotten better if the Meet Director had not felt the need. Ed Bowes saw the set-up and wanted to know what was going on. Eddie John Denny was talking fast but what he said was not in Bowes's contract.

At the encouragement of the on duty police Eddie John Denny made a sizable donation to the Loughlin Spiked Shoe Club and was shown the door. Word of the scam spread, a reputation was made and another Armory myth was born.

Under "Accomplishments" I doubt Eddie John Denny had the Loughlin Games on his Manhattan application. Had it not been for his sense of humor Eddie John Denny would probably have graduated from Manhattan a proud alum with a great job as an engineer or accountant. But then, would Rhino have ever spoken?

Humor, like beauty, is in the eye of the beholder. *The Texas Chainsaw Massacre* is one of Hollywood's all-time B flicks. It is a frightening idea, but millions of people have derived pleasure watching orchestrated mutilation. There is a certain shock value that is nonpareil.

Understanding shock value Eddie John Denny arrived early for the campus screening of *The Texas Chainsaw Massacre*. He decided to camp out in the first row. By the third murder everyone was past gruesome and on to comparison. Sometimes life copies art.

The Texas Chainsaw Massacre had a cultist appeal and drew a big crowd. Without warning or cue Eddie John Denny pulled a 12" mini chain saw from under his seat. Oiled and lubricated it took two pulls to start. Masked and saw buzzing Eddie John Denny jumped to the stage. By the third rev the theater was half empty. Within two minutes the faint odor of urine was detectable. Rhino Rothberg, the top 800m high school kid in the country, on his senior recruiting trip to Manhattan never saw the end of the movie. It is a small world.

Two days later Eddie John Denny sat alone, unmasked in front of the Dean of Students. Ten minutes later he was no longer a Manhattan student. His defense was that it was only a joke. The verdict and opinion stated that a good comedian does not have to explain his humor.

Randy ROTC rose to shake Eddie John Denny's hand and told him he was, "Damn glad to meet him." Rhino had spoken and somehow life would never be the same.

THUMB TACKS

Eddie John Denny was bumming. His Fleet Feet Package Service was headed for the rocks. It was going to be a dry Saturday night at Villanova. The only answer Eddie John Denny had for anyone was a snappy "No!" There was no service and there was no smile.

"Find a need and fill it." Randy ROTC liked to repeat, find a need and fill it — the secret to success. Eddie John Denny was only on campus a week before he realized the "inconvenience of being 18 in a 21 state." It took another week, a job at the Ardmore A&P and he was in business.

Eddie John Denny was a whip on the cash register. The big deal was access. It was the beer. He recruited Mickey to help with carrying and together they had an unlimited supply of Bud, Miller and Rolling Rock. Within a month he was the "Beer Man on Campus."

Eddie John Denny's ship had come in.

As the wizard of cash register number two the challenge of the job soon left him. On the off times he would call for price checks. He would catch one of the high school kids stocking shelves and boom over the intercom, "Is Prince Albert in a can?" Or he would request that someone check to see if the store's butcher had "pig's feet." When Sal Monella was paged from the deli the manager had heard enough. The inmates would not run his asylum.

In certain terms Eddie John Denny was told that his next mistake would be his last. Weighing the rewards of his recent comedic past against the prospects of an endless cycle of wet weekends Eddie John Denny shelved the humor, accepted a demotion to the stock room and funneled the beer through Mickey's register.

For the better part of a month Eddie John Denny was a citizen. He would joke at the table that his Bud stock had risen two points since his Fleet Feet Package Service had begun. He wondered aloud how much one of those "big houses" on the Tennis Courts cost?

The intercom in the stock room was poor. The static and cackles blurred with the sound of squeaking wheels and idle conversation making price checks unintelligible. He did the best he could.

The Main Line of suburban Philadelphia is one of the most exclusive areas in the country. Excellent service is not so much courtesy as a God given right. Mickey came from a back woods town in Massachusetts. Tact and social graces were skills yet unlearned.

"Register three; price check...Tampax..." The message faded out in the stockroom. Eddie John Denny was up, laid his sticker gun down and headed off to hardware, aisle two.

In a flash he was at Mickey's register and found an impeccably dressed middle aged woman and her blossoming blonde-haired, blue-eyed daughter. He had two boxes in his hands and with all the sincerity of an honest mistake asked, "Do you want the kind you push in with your thumb or the ones you need a hammer for?"

On his way to the register Eddie John Denny thought about the inventor of thumb tacks. How much was that patent worth? Thumb tacks — find a need and fill it — the secret to success.

Mickey's jaw hit the floor. The 16 year old turned a crimson red and her mother screamed for the manager. Profuse apologies did little for damage control. Eddie John Denny and Mickey were fired on the spot. The lady was given her groceries and her Tampax free. Eddie John Denny offered to help take them to her car. The manager pointed to the door and yelled, "Out!"

Thumb tacks — maybe Napoleon should have listened to Tallyrand when he said: "You can do everything with thumb tacks, except sit on them." Eddie John Denny sat alone, high and dry, marooned on the rocks, "No, no, no! I didn't get your stuff." There was water, water everywhere, but not a drop for drink.

INSECURITY

It was always Weasel this or Weasel that; it was never Officer Rizzo. Randy ROTC pleaded with the Weasel. Randy had gotten snagged trying to smuggle a quart of milk out of the lunch room. The Weasel was going to teach Randy a lesson and pour the milk down the drain. Randy guiltily protested the waste of food. Randy would not let the bottle go. The Weasel tugged. The bottle slipped and smashed on the floor. There was milk everywhere.

Randy was indignant. He pointed to the floor and angrily yelled something about people starving. The Weasel looked at the mess on the floor. What a mess.

From the table Shep heard the crash, saw the milk and the argument. He stood and yelled to Randy, "No use crying over spilled milk!" and sat down. The humor was lost on Randy. Shep got a huge laugh at the table.

On a roll Shep did his impression of Dustin Hoffman as Ratso Rizzo, "If it's free...then I ain't stealing!" and he wiggled his nose up in the air like a mouse. We died laughing.

The Weasel was a mid-level flunky on the campus security force. He was a shirt tail relative of Frank Rizzo, Philly's ex-Police Chief Mayor with the 8th grade education and the diction to prove it.

The Weasel's main job was tickets and towing. Getting a car on campus was like getting through Check Point Charlie. Keeping a car on campus was simply impossible. The Weasel was good at his job.

As a political appointee the Weasel understood how things worked. Rumors persisted that Howard Porter, Villanova's most recent addition to the NBA used to put a sign on his car windshield, "This is Howard Porter's car." Howard's car never got ticketed. Howard's car never got towed. Howard had friends. The Weasel understood "friends."

Security bought Weasel a new car. The car was solid white, unmarked. Was the Weasel going undercover? For several weeks he was on a slow cruise looking sharp in his white car, handing out tickets and calling the tow truck. A tow would definitely crimp the finances. Forty five dollars was a lot of cheese steaks and milk shakes. The guy in the tow truck had a heart of stone. Once that hook was on the car, it was forty five dollars gone.

Eddie John Denny had a '67 Chevy Impala with a three toot horn that said, "Look at me!" He called it the "War Wagon." He had bought it from a little old lady in New Paltz, no rust, no scratches and the heater worked. One Sunday night he brought a new dresser from home. He parked the car in front of his dorm to unload. When he came back the car was gone.

Immediately Eddie John Denny thought someone was pulling a joke. He patted his pockets for keys. He had his keys. His car was gone. In a second he was frantic. He ran around the dorm, no car. And then he saw the Weasel's white car parked by the Pie Shoppe. The Weasel was on his 9 o'clock coffee break.

Eddie John Denny found the Weasel meditating over a cup of coffee. Before he ever said a word the Weasel raised his hand and said, "I had it towed." He did not even look at Eddie John Denny.

Eddie John Denny began to mutter, "You stupid son of..." The Weasel raised his head and cut Eddie John Denny off mid sentence, "What was that...Chainsaw?" We all have our reputations.

The Highway Patrol was one of the more popular television shows of our childhood. Broderick Crawford had a name and a gravely voice that established police work as a manly profession. Every episode ended with a conviction. Crawford always got his man. There should be such resolution in life.

One night while the Weasel sat in the Pie Shoppe with his coffee and donuts someone got a stencil and spray painted "Highway Patrol" on the side of his new white car. It was a messy job. There were drips and black dots all over the side of the car. The investigation lasted two weeks. There were interviews and alibis. Eddie John Denny had been at his work study job in the Library. He was called in three times anyway. He never "cracked" or wavered from his story. At the table he was indignant.

Randy sat silent for days on end. Randy sat silent on his hands. The cat had his tongue. He was never suspected and he never got interviewed. It took three days for the Weasel to get his car repainted. It took Randy three weeks to get the black stuff out from under his fingernails.

THE ROVER BOYS

My legs hurt, Jackson was in a foul mood, and Ian mentioned something about survival tactics. We weren't at the Cabrini mixer 30 seconds when it was apparent we had made a mistake. There were only three women in the room and two were college nuns. There would be no dancing tonight.

Mickey, Charlie Checkers and Eddie John Denny had just finished a stirring rendition of The Who's "My Generation." They congratulated each other and gave a few wolf cheers into the air. In the confined space of a converted hallway they were loud, very loud.

Jack looked at me and asked, "You know why The Who sang that song?"

Jackson always had the little tidbits that made life more interesting. I thought it must be the Beatles. I said nothing, just shrugged.

Without looking he pointed towards Mickey, Charlie and Eddie John Denny, "The Who sing that song so assholes like that," his arm bolted straight, "wouldn't."

Ouch, Jack was in a very foul mood.

Mickey was out of ear shot but he was too drunk to care anyway. His beer cup teetered dangerously on his right hip. His body swayed like a racket. It was anybody's guess which would hit the floor first. Mickey gave those nuns a 1000 yard stare and what he was thinking could only get him in trouble with the Pope or St. Peter.

Mickey raised his arm and blasted, "Red Rover, Red Rover, I dare anything to come over!"

For a second no one moved. I heard but I did not believe. Jack turned to me with a, "You've got to be kidding," look on his face.

Mid sway Mickey boomed again, "Red Rover, Red Rover, I dare anything to come over!"

The nuns looked at Mickey. He had their attention. What he was going to do with it was anybody's guess. I was afraid to think.

Charlie and Eddie John Denny began to half tackle Mickey. The beer cup went flying. They dragged Mickey to the door. His resistance was real and his challenge persisted. "Red Rover, Red Rover..." the sound got muffled as Mickey disappeared through the door.

I shook my head at Jack. Ian wanted to know who Red Rover was. Jack drained his beer, "I'm ready," and we were off. The best thing about this night would be brunch the next morning. Mickey had just loaded Johnny Puma's gun and pointed it at himself.

That Sunday Mickey was late for the brunch. Space was made for him at the table. Mickey ate quietly, self absorbed in his breakfast and hangover.

Johnny Puma waited and waited like a cat for a rat and broke the long silence with a simple question, "A nun...?" And without cue we began to laugh. The cat was all over the rat again.

OF RAIN AND PARADES

Randy ROTC was desperate. When Randy got desperate he twisted his neck left and lifted his chin like his collar was too tight. Randy was wearing a T-shirt. He stood at the bend of the glass enclosed ramp, desperate. A girl followed him. Nobody missed the girl. She was tall and thin with blue eyes and long straight blonde hair. She was a beauty. She was a nine o'clock girl.

Randy came to the table with his tray. There was desperation in his voice. He began to talk, stopping mid sentence to twist his head left and lift his chin. He begged us not to say anything to her. He was dying.

"Please guys, I'll never ask you to do anything like this again... please don't rain on my parade."

She stood alone and impatient by the napkins. She was from a Beach Boy song. Midway through a Frolic Randy had told me about her. He used terms like, "the girl of my dreams," "everything a man could want," "she makes my heart flutter..." It was a long half hour home for me. And there she stood, fidgeting by the napkins.

Randy's pleas were met with silence. He left his tray, turned and walked to the girl. He lead her to the table.

"Guys, I'd like to introduce Pam to you." Individually, on cue we rose, mumbled how nice it was to meet her and sat down. Pam smiled and nodded. Then she sat down.

"Randall has spoken so much about you all. I feel that I almost know some of you," she beamed.

Not quite, I thought...Randall? I saw more than a glint in a few people's eyes. Believe me, it took a lot of compassion to let that one go. And some of us were experiencing compassion for the first time.

Johnny Puma asked Randall how physics was going. Randall described the quantum leap a positron had made and how excited he was with the experiment. Pam mentioned that Randall had won the school's science fair with his sixth grade project on potatoes.

Potatoes? Mr. Potatohead! Could I let that go? I ached. I looked at Randall, Mr. Potatohead. I looked at Pam. I looked back at Randall, compassion, I had compassion.

And then there was a rap. Eddie John Denny pounded his fist twice on the glass. All heads turned. Eddie John Denny smiled and kept walking. If we did not stop him he was going to be himself and ruin everything. Dark clouds loomed on the horizon.

Shep tried to intercept Eddie John Denny at the silverware. Eddie John Denny smiled and blew past him to the table. Eddie John Denny dropped his tray in the last open spot and headed off to the milk machine. Shep followed Eddie John Denny to the milk machine. Eddie John Denny was in no mood to talk to Shep. He spun on his heel and returned. He did not seem to notice the girl.

He did notice everyone's icy stares. He could not figure it out. He raised his head and gave two quick sniffs and said, "Why is everyone looking at me? I didn't do it!"

Eddie John Denny poked the tip of his spoon into his soup and asked the table, "Does this black thing look like it has a wing?"

There was more silence. The stares intensified.

He looked at Randy and the girl and back to Randy.

"You know Randy, I've got to hand it to you, everytime I see you, you're with another beautiful girl."

Eddie John Denny smiled and laughed and stopped because nobody else did.

Clouds, clouds and then lightning

...OWH SCATMAN!

Eddie John Denny could be in an absolute funk, excitedly reliving the conquest of his latest Rosemonster or deep into the details of his latest scam ("This one is going to work!"). All Duke had to say was "...owh, Scatman!"

Eddie John Denny would stop, turn to Duke and point, "He was gonna win. You know he was gonna win!" Duke would laugh. He loved to push that button.

Breakfast, lunch or dinner, it could have been anytime in the dining hall at Villanova. All somebody had to do was mention The Armory and the stories would flow. Duke would make this drawn out "owh" noise and pipe in "...Scatman!" Eddie John Denny would reflexively shoot back his reply and then get quiet. Everyone knew his story.

Coach Frier would take us to the Armory on a van for one of the January stampedes put on by the old Metropolitan AAU. Ten minutes after arriving at the Armory Eddie John Denny would spread his arms, look to the ceiling and start to wax romantic about being in the homeland. I told him I saw his face on a "not wanted" poster by the front door. He didn't think that was funny, but everybody else did.

Eddie John Denny would lead us off to some distant section in the balcony. He would trudge down the aisle to his favorite seat. The ground under his feet was crunchy. "Look!" He would point to the floor, "The remnants of someone's lost lunch — mummified!" For a second we thought he was kidding, but then again, considering this was the Armory, maybe not.

Save for the two mile or a possible invite, all the races were handicaps. Your handicap was based on your seed time, real or imagined. Seeding was on the honor system, which was not much of a system and had little to do with honor. You told the clerk the time you thought you would run and got assigned a spot on the track. The good guys started from scratch. In theory everyone had a chance to win, and in fact the liars always did.

Duke won the two mile in close to nine minutes. Everyone else had representative efforts and got a chance to blow out some carbon against some competition.

"The 300! Hey guys, the 300!" Eddie John Denny was on his feet. The 300 came at the end of a long program. Everybody was done. Eddie John Denny had been betting dimes with different guys for race winners throughout the night. He talked us all into throwing a dime into the hat, winner take all.

There were seven or eight heats in the 300, easily 15 guys in each race. With a gun start the guys in the 300 were off in a flurry around the track like leaves in a whirl wind. For 30 seconds it was a dog race with no rabbit. It was in the final heat that Eddie John Denny recognized Scatman.

"That's Scatman! He was sectional champ in the 100 and 200. He's gonna win!"

We watched a few starts. Yes, Scatman was quick, but, and it was a prohibitive but, he was starting from scratch, and the scratch guys never won. They never got into the race. Eddie John Denny announced, "I got Scatman." Everyone figured he had a loser.

Scatman wore red. Eddie John Denny was on his chair screaming "Scatman, Scatman!" and suddenly all we could see was a red streak dodging the handicapped, zooming through the crowd like a hot knife through butter.

Scatman held a tight corner and came off the turn destined for victory. He had one guy to catch and 80 yards to do it. No one cared for their dime. A scratch guy was going to win the 300! Everyone was yelling, "...owh, Scatman!" and then...POW!

This little girl saw the leader pass, looked left and stepped right in front of the Scatman. There was no time to react. This was combined, coupled motion. The little girl made ground contact in the next zip code while Scatman crashed and burned on the Armory floor.

Eddie John Denny sank to his seat with a thump. Another unsuccessful Armory gambling junket. "Jesus," he said to no one in particular, "he woulda won." Woulda, shoulda, coulda, the gambler's laments...owh, Scatman!

WHERE THERE ARE COWS

Jackson Rash came to Villanova to run. He had saved his money the last two years of high school and had enough for one semester. He gambled that he would land an ROTC scholarship in the fall. If not? Life after Villanova would soon follow.

Mid week Jack trained alone during a morning break so he could march ROTC in the afternoons. Coach Frier approached him this day and asked if he would not be so kind as to take one of the top Kenyan runners out for a run. The Kenyan was burning up the indoor circuit and just wanted to get in some miles. Jack could only nod in awe.

Jack came from somewhere next to nowhere in the west. Actually it was a small island off the coast of Seattle in Puget Sound. He told me it was the island where the Great Imposter lived. I said, "Tony Curtis?" He got mad and said, "No! The real Great Impostor!"

And now he was out on the Frolic with the Olympic Gold Medalist. The Kenyan spoke the Queen's English to a 'T.' Jack said they began at a comfortable pace. They shared stories of home and the conversation never lagged. They hit the first pasture. A number of cows grazed indifferently off in the pasture. Jack's new friend became agitated. His eyes scanned the pastures. His pace quickened. The conversation stopped.

Jack did his best to hang on. The Kenyan flashed furtive looks left and right and continued his charge. Jack began to fade. He was good, but he was not great.

Falling behind Jack called out, "What's going on?" The Kenyan pointed to the cows and signaled for them to continue. Jack replied, "Cows, those are cows! They won't hurt you!"

The Kenyan, whose ancestors were herders and rustlers, knew cows, "Yes cows...and where there are cows there are lions!"

Jack looked around the table and laughed at his own story. He had this innocent "isn't that unbelievable" look on his face. Everyone stared at him in silence wondering if it was a joke. Shep had little wonder.

Shep, our resident cow expert from New York City, the man who once wondered himself if cows bit, barked, "Yeah, where there are cows there is bullshit...and you are full of it!"

Jack sat stunned. I looked at him and gave him a friendly shrug. Someday, I thought, it would make a great story.

THE MAN FROM JAPAN

Jackson Rash was my best friend. It didn't matter where we were or what we were doing, we always had something to talk about.

We were so different. He came from a small town where everybody knew everybody. Every team he played on was made up of his brothers. He played basketball against American Indians. Real Indians.

Jackson was not just good at sports. Jackson was smart. After I got a D- on an English paper he taught me how to write. I can still hear Jackson say, "Simple sentences, write in simple sentences." Subject, verb, predicate.

Jackson could also sing. He was in the choir that Jim Croce belonged to. Jackson could sing and play the guitar and he had women like a dog has fleas. Jackson was the man from Japan.

The only problem with Jack's women is that most of them were big, very big. One night at the table Mickey said, "Where there are cows, there is Jackson!" Shep laughed and started right in, tag team.

"Jackson," Shep's tongue was razor sharp, "You need a leash or a license to date that woman from Good Council?"

Mickey asked Shep, "You mean Hunkanova?" and then turning to Jack, "Hunkanova, Indian for 'she who blocks the sun.'"

Jack took the beating like a man and Shep got personal, "You making love to her?"

Mickey supplied the "how-to" answer, "Roll her in flour and go for the wet spot!"

The table roared. Randy ROTC got it. Rhino shook his head. Duke fought back a smile. I felt bad for Jack. He just kept nodding his head, "You guys are pretty funny."

The tag team kept up their routine and laughed everytime one of them mentioned "flour" or "Hunkanova." Jack continued to force a smile, finish his meal and then he left.

Mickey thought he had Jack's number. Every chance he got he took a shot at Jack. Flour, Hunkanova or cows, the jokes never stopped being funny for Mickey or Shep. They stopped being funny for everyone else.

Jack showed up one morning on the Bricks. Mickey started right in. Jack ignored Mickey for a second then asked if we wanted to see a magic trick. We were up for a trick.

Jack volunteered Mickey to be his straight man. Jack pulled a white dandelion puff ball off the grass. He broke a piece off the stem and gave it to Mickey. "Hide it anywhere on your body, anywhere." Jack closed his eyes and turned his back. Mickey stuck the stem in his shoe.

Jack faced Mickey and used the puff ball like a piece of radar tracing Mickey's legs and arms finally stopping at his mouth. Jack said, "It's in your mouth!" with great excitement.

"Not even close!" was Mickey's equally excited reply.

Jack persisted, "It's under your tongue. Let me see!"

Let me see. Just to prove Jack the fool Mickey stuck out his tongue. Without a second's hesitation Jack planted the seeds of thought in Mickey's mouth proving for all to see that in "Jack's World of Magic" the hand is quicker than the tongue. One down.

Shep missed the magic. Mickey sulked for days. There were no more "cow" commentaries from him. Mickey lived and let live.

Shep may have missed the magic but at the next party he did not miss the blonde. No one did. Jack showed up with a drop dead blonde that nobody could forget. When he got out his guitar to sing, we all did too, jockeying to get close just to smell her.

Jack was a master. He hung that blonde out like shark bait just to see who would snap. Everybody did. And when Shep was introduced the astonished blonde looked at Jack knowingly and said, "Oh...the shower singer!"

The "shower singer" was not funny, yet, to anyone except Jack and the blonde. No one else had a clue. And before anyone could ask, Jack was strumming his guitar and wailing about an Oreo cookie. Shep shrugged it all off and left.

But Shep's memory of the blonde lingered on. The next day at the table Shep quizzed Jack, "What the hell is a girl like that doing with you?" Shep fired a few more barbs about Jack's singing. Mickey, having officially retired, had nothing to say. Jack spooned his soup to the end and rose to leave.

"Hey Shep," Jack said, dead serious, "I read a study about singing." Jack talked fast, "And they said that 20% of the men in America jerk off in the shower," Jack shot right through, "while the other 80% sing," and then with strong emphasis Jack asked, "You know *what* they sing?"

Shep had no idea and stated bluntly, "I could care less."

Jack half-smiled, "You must have your hands full then," and he full smiled as we filled in the blanks for Shep, the "Shower Singer" loud and clear.

THE POWER OF A MAN

Philly is a sports town. The people that live there understand, appreciate and support their teams. Philly is the home of the Liberty Bell, Independence Hall and Ben Franklin. There is a certain passion and respect the natives are brought up with. There is an in born sense of history.

The Philly Track Classic was one of the gems of the Eastern Indoor Track Circuit. For six or seven weekends throughout the winter the larger arenas on the East Coast were filled with spectators to watch the best college, Olympic hopefuls and national champs battle it out.

This night was different, it was a two-for-one. After the meet would be a simulcast of "The Fight." Over a life time one becomes jaded to the hype of "The Fight," it becomes a cliché. This fight never was and never will be a cliché.

Closed circuit television was in its infancy. The Spectrum was filled to capacity by men to watch TV. After the meet would be the simulcast of the second Ali v. Frazier fight from New York. This was the most publicized event of the 20th century. And Joe Frazier was from Philadelphia.

The last event of the meet was the mile. Duke had run fourth in a field that included Liquori, Dave Wottle, Tony Waldrop and Barry Brown. Villanova had won the distance medley and the two mile relay. Good times were posted in the individual events. The meet ended and we moved to the pole vault pits to get a good seat. Everyone else had the same idea. Soon there was no place to sit, so we stood.

Joe Frazier was from Philly. Joe Frazier could not run and Joe Frazier did not hide. Joe Frazier was like an old telephone pole, proud, black and splintered. What you saw is what you got. Looks were not deceiving. Style, strength or cleverness could not do what an ax would.

Muhammad Ali was the greatest. Eloquent and articulate Ali's mental acuity rivaled the gladiator skill. Of the southern lineage of Henry Clay, Ali assumed a posture that was loved, hated, feared or pitied, without compromise. Ali was the greatest. His time had come.

Henry Luce recorded the epic events of Life and Time and Sports Illustrated with this bout. Everyone in America had an opinion. This was the biggest fight of all time. The consciousness of America was focused.

I remember little of the fight until the 10th round. I remember the chant. It started like a faint heartbeat, a faint tapping. It was certain and deliberate and got louder and louder until it was all you could hear. I chanted with the crowd at a TV screen, "Ali...Ali." He had to hear.

The tragedy in boxing lies not in the graphic death by knockout but rather the erosion of skill, disarmed by Time, yesterday's diminished hero is paraded from one spectacle to the next championed by past feats, forever scarred by defeats.

Ali v. Frazier, the two strata of Black America. Frazier was what the black man was, Ali, what the black man could be. The future v. the past, like an angry conscience they struggled. Style and glory v. reality and grit. Muhammad Ali was the greatest, to take on all comers and Time. We meant no disrespect to Joe Frazier, the hometown boy, but we chanted louder, "Ali...Ali.

THE FORGOTTEN ZONE

People seldom improve when they have no other model but themselves to copy. For young men spoiled with talent, the realities of life may be no more complicated than placing one foot in front of the other. I know now that Jumbo Elliott realized this.

For many people on the team Jumbo remained an enigma during their career at Villanova. The true "stars" were occasionally privileged with his words of wisdom but to all Jumbo remained a figure distant and unapproachable. Never knowing the man I cannot say if this was by design or due to a reticent personality. One was taught by the older runners. It was an apprentice program of sorts. The teachers would periodically change but somehow you learned what counted.

The last days leading up to the Indoor IC4A Championships were filled with good cheer. Everyone seemed well satisfied with their performances to date. The levity of the locker room crept onto the boards. Somebody put snow in Shep's spikes. There was a snowball fight on one of the warm-up runs. Our focus drifted in spite of our workload. The immediacy of the moment escaped us. The coming IC4A Championship meet was just "another race."

Princeton was a short hour's drive north. We packed the van and jokingly loaded up with little regard for the task at hand. Once everyone was there Assistant Coach Frier started the van and our journey began. Jumbo would meet us there. With a 6 p.m. meet start our noon departure would give us plenty of time to relax and unwind from the trip. Nobody paid much attention to where Frier was going, after all the years he had been a coach he could get to Jadwin Gym on autopilot. So we thought.

The van chatter hardly stopped the first time someone asked Frier if he was lost. The road and suddenly the neighborhood were quickly changing from bad to worse. We were driving through the part of some city the Chamber of Commerce tried to forget.

Frier mumbled he was "following directions" and we drove on. March can be cold and gray and this was a perfect March day. The neighborhood was crumbled bricks and burnt out buildings. Somebody asked Frier a second time if he knew where he was going.

"We're meeting Jumbo...somewhere," and he looked at a little slip of paper that had directions, put it back in his coat pocket and drove on.

Five minutes later he pulled up to the curb behind Jumbo's El Dorado. Jumbo was standing alone, his hands were in his pockets and his breathe was white from the cold. He stood a solitary figure against a backdrop of urban desolation. Frier ordered everyone out. Wherever we were it sure was not Princeton.

The five story brick building had "Infirmary" etched into the stone above the keystone. The cornerstone was dated 1872. The immediate neighborhood had a bar on one corner, a corner grocery with a metal gate and two buildings that were burnt out shells. There were no trees. The street was a pock marked blacktop stained with bubble gum and littered with broken glass. The nozzle cap of a rusted fire hydrant hung casually on a rusted chain.

Charlie Checkers said, "This isn't the Twilight Zone, this is the Forgotten Zone."

Everyone looked around in silence wondering what we were doing here.

Jumbo and Frier talked a minute then Frier said, "Let's go!" and he and Jumbo led us up the concrete steps of the Infirmary.

The reek of urine was immediate. It was a stench. We marched on but the stench did not abate. There was nobody there to direct us, we followed up and up a staircase to the fourth floor. The heat was suffocating the higher we walked. Our top coats were off and we were sweating. It had to be 95 degrees, it had to be.

We waited on the fourth floor until everyone finished the climb. Nobody knew what was going on or where we were or what we were doing. Somebody noted the time and wished we were at the hotel. I breathed the hot air and loosened my tie. I was sweating through my shirt.

Frier broke the silence, "Listen up! We are only going to be here a short while. There are some people that would like to meet you. Please follow Jumbo into the room."

We filed into a room, maybe 20'x20' to see 12 people God never created. They were on wheelchairs and wheeled stretchers all twisted and flinching. The heat, the smell, the human agony; I could feel myself getting flushed. I needed some fresh air. I could not figure out what was going on. I found a chair and sat.

I refused to look at my teammates. One guy in a wheelchair caught my eye. He stared right into my eyes. He looked at everybody. He looked like a bird. He had a big head and his chin rested on his chest. His legs hung over the seat like a cloth doll. His hands were little gnarled balls. I dropped my head. I could not figure out why they had brought us here, whatever the reason, it was not a good idea.

Jumbo introduced a thin, middle aged black lady. I did not pay close attention. He then individually introduced each of us and noted our accomplishments to date. I remember thinking that I was in another world.

The black lady thanked us for coming and told us how much it meant to her patients to meet the best runners in the world. Somehow that title did not mean too much right then.

She went on to introduce each patient and tell us a little about him and what were some of his dreams. I looked around the room at the pictureless pale green walls and kept saying to myself that their dreams were not going to happen in this lifetime. The black lady finished and asked if we would not mind answering some questions. We were silent.

She took the hand of the guy that looked like a bird into her palm. One word at a time the gnarled fingers signed out, "What—is—it—like—to—run—fast?"

Nobody said anything. I could feel the blood pulsing in my ears. My nose started to run. Jumbo picked Duke. He was our captain, our best runner, our leader.

Duke cleared his throat, raised his chin and began, "We all have different talents in life..." I do not remember anything else. I was cursing myself. There was a twitch in my chin. I could not believe this was happening. Tears were rolling down my cheeks. I did not care who saw it. I was never so glad in my life to be who I was.

It was cold in the van ride to Princeton but no one complained. Two hours later we were on the floor at Jadwin Gym. We knew why we were there.

That Saturday night it was quiet on the van ride home. There was not the type of celebration you would expect. On paper the meet had been a great success — 12 seasonal bests, nine personal bests, three IC4A individual champions and the IC4A Indoor Team Championship. It was not that we had done anything special, just what our special talents allowed us to do. Sometimes the greatest lessons in life are taught unspoken.

THE WHAT FOR

The Field House Zoo Parties were given to excess and some were more excessive than others. The 40 or 50 kegs were a chance for the local beverage centers to clean out old or unpopular brands. The music was loud, the beer warm, the gym was hot and there was always a big crowd. Life could not get much better than this.

The Jersey guys would go nuts when a band from the Jersey Shore — two words spoken with reverence — showed up and did the "E Street Shuffle." All I remember was this bearded guy with long hair jumping back and forth on stage like he was Chuck Berry. Personally, I liked to hear the Black guy play the sax. He could play. Who would ever have thought that the bearded guy would someday be The Boss?

Eddie John Denny had more than a few too many. For a scant moment he stood at the center of a large circle to catch his breath. He chugged another beer. One way or another the end was near. I kept my distance.

Eddie John Denny threw his cup of beer to the floor. He began to spin like a helicopter, then zoomed around a circle like a plane. As a Russian Cossack he spent more time on the floor. Everyone laughed. As Eddie John Denny tried to right himself he staggered left and crashed into the crowd. He sprayed beer all over Hughie O'Kane.

Hughie O'Kane was a loser. He showed up in the locker room one afternoon, assumed a three point stance and charged. The team was half in a jock, bodies bounced like bowling pins, no one knew what hit them.

There was a lot of "What the fuck?" and "Son of a bitch!" -ing going on. As the team righted itself Hughie O'Kane stood at the other end of the hallway laughing. He slowly lowered himself in another three point stance when Shep boomed out from the end of the line.

"C'mon mother fucker, do it again!" It was more an invitation than a challenge. In each hand Shep held his Adidas Meteors, the shoes he had run 1:46 point in that summer, the shoes with the ¾" spikes.

We rummaged our lockers. Spikes clicked the metal walls. We agreed with Shep, to a man we told Hughie O'Kane to, "Do it again."

Hughie O'Kane was a teenage bully from a coal town in western Pennsylvania. At 6'2", 200 pounds he had held sway in high school. He was no longer "big man on campus." Assessing the odds he slowly rose from his three point stance, gave us the finger and walked out the back door, mad.

Hughie O'Kane played football. Everyone on the football team hated him. His nickname was "the practice dummy." He was always starting fights. He even fought with Jake. He called Jake an "asshole." And Eddie John Denny had just sprayed beer all over Hughie O'Kane.

Eddie John Denny had no clue. He tried to stagger back to the center of the circle but Hughie O'Kane grabbed his arm. There was a muted curse and a sucker punch that dropped Eddie John Denny in a heartbeat.

Eddie John Denny drunkenly rolled on the floor. Hughie O'Kane delivered two swift kicks before anyone could get close enough to push him away. Eddie John Denny lay in a clump on the floor. The damage was done.

Amid the noise of the Field House Zoo party no one noticed Eddie John Denny. He was unconscious. Someone ran for security. Blood ran from Eddie John Denny.

The trip to the emergency room seemed to take hours. Eddie John Denny was groggy. He thought he lost three teeth. He was right. He kept spitting out chips. He could not take a deep breathe, he had two broken ribs. His left eye was swollen shut.

Eddie John Denny did not show to the table until Tuesday. He was living on toast and milk. He had a huge black eye, but he was received as a bit of a hero because we all figured that this incident would surely get Hughie O'Kane bounced from school.

We were wrong. The fire in Eddie John Denny was diminished. He had made the decision not to go to the Dean. He cited his Manhattan trouble. "I don't have the best track record, see?" Disappointedly we saw. He did not want to chance himself getting suspended for provoking a fight.

We did not agree but we understood, except for Ian. Ian got mad. "If he ever touches me," Ian blurted out to no one in particular, "I'll give him the fookin' what for!"

This was spoken with great conviction. I happened to catch a sly smile creep onto Duke's face as Ian spoke. Was the Duke laughing at him or did he know something about the "what for?" I dismissed it as an Irish thing.

But "what for?" struck me. I looked at a quiet Eddie John Denny dipping his toast in a cup of milk and painfully letting it dissolve in his mouth. What for?

THE LOSER

To begin with Ian was not in a good mood. He never liked to lose. In reality he did not lose. He had gotten a "B" just like I had promised him. He did not understand symbolism then and he did not care to understand symbolism now. He grudgingly put a five dollar bill and a few crumpled ones on the counter. He ignored my conversation, "Hey Tony," he said, "Is it pizza yet?"

"Ian, don't you see? It was the gun in the first act," I knew what I was talking about. "Ibsen used the gun to forecast that something bad would happen." Ian slowly turned and stared at me. He did not see. More importantly, he did not care. I put Hedda Gabbler to rest.

Tony the Parrot swung open the pizza door and parroted. "It is NOT pizza yet!" with special emphasis on "not."

Ian seemed disgusted. I was not going to let it ruin my night, my free pizza. I had made out like a bandit. Not only was I getting a free pizza, Ian gave me $10. worth of Pie Shoppe tickets he had squirreled away for five bucks. What a deal!

Impatiently Tony the Parrot swung open the oven door and parroted, "It is NOT pizza yet!" There was special mastery of "not."

Tony the Parrot was just "off the boat." Tony the Parrot's vocabulary was limited to what you said and "son of a bitch." He used "son of a bitch" like he used air, but Tony the Parrot still had the best pizza on the Main Line.

Simple pleasures are sometimes the greatest. A Saturday night six cut at Tony's could be a satisfying meal or a great late night snack. My pizza was free. It was my payment for "helping" Ian on the Ibsen Paper. Simplicity is the spice of life.

The bell at the front door jingled. Hughie O'Kane followed the jingle. I cursed my luck. Ian turned and glared. He never took his eyes of Hughie O'Kane.

"What are you two girls up to?" was Hughie O'Kane's opening insult.

I told Ian to ignore him. Ian did not hear. He stood transfixed. I tried to get him to turn around. He shrugged my hand off his shoulder. Hughie O'Kane swaggered closer.

"An Irish fuck!" Hughie O'Kane seemed to delight in his discovery. "How come you Irish bastards don't go back to your own country?" The beer had not enhanced Hughie O'Kane's diplomacy or eloquence, "Who wants you?" His taunts continued crude and pointless.

Ian seethed. The pot did not like the kettle calling it black. His focus was unblinking on Hughie O'Kane's face. Ian's steel blue eyes were wide, hard and cold. Hughie O'Kane came closer to Ian than he should have.

I said, "Hey Tony, is it pizza yet?" Tony the Parrot alone in his world swung open the oven door, shook his head and said, "It is not pizza yet," still emphasizing "not." I told him to hurry up.

I felt a hand on my arm, "What's your hurry Bonebag?"

Ian pushed the hand off my arm. I turned diplomatically and said, "Look guy, we're not looking for any trouble." I began to say something else when Ian told me to shut up.

In the background Tony the Parrot swung open the oven door and announced, "It is now pizza!" There was special mastery of "now." He slid the pizza on a tray, cut it and slid the tray on the counter. To get our attention he proudly announced, "It is now pizza!" and now no one cared.

"Shut up?" Hughie O'Kane raised his eyebrows. "What...are you a tough guy?" Out weighed and undersized the smart money was on Hughie. But you cannot measure will with a yardstick just as you can't weigh it with a scale. Hughie O'Kane put his finger on Ian's chest. Ian's focus was fixed. For a silent second he stared and stared and then struck like a cobra.

Hughie O'Kane was through. He staggered two steps and then he dropped in a heartbeat. His nose was split from eye to eye. Red oozed, then ran from his face. Ian stepped forward and taunted him to rise. It was classic Clay v. Liston. The power of a man. There was no response from Hughie O'Kane.

What Tony the Parrot had to say and all began and ended with "son of a bitch." He bellowed "son of a bitch" as he struggled to climb over the counter. I grabbed Ian. Again he shrugged me off. Ian turned, took the pizza from the counter and flung it at Hughie. Splat, pizza to go...and we were gone.

The run lasted two blocks. Ian slowed to a walk, then stopped. A trickle of blood had run into his eye. He leaned forward and dabbed his face. He slowly rose pointing his finger to me. I pointed my finger at him and this time I beat him to the punch, "the fookin' what for!" I said, with a half laugh, pleased at my own recognition.

"No!" Ian countered, now in a good mood. "I hit him with the Hedda right on the fookin' Gabbler!" We both laughed.

And in the dim of the street lights Ian dabbed at his forehead. There was the slightest tremor of his hand. Tested and not found wanting he looked determined down Lancaster Pike. Hughie O'Kane had mistaken the size of the fight in the dog. Hughie O'Kane was still a loser, but he finally got a brain. And he never bothered us again.

A SLIP OF THE LIP

Mickey laughed like a devil. It seemed of little concern to him that Johnny Puma was trying to choke the life out of him. Mickey's eyes only got bigger as he croaked the best he could, "Salt...salt...salt."

And every "salt" burned the wound. Johnny's lunge over the table had sent all lunches flying. It took a moment for anyone to react. Johnny already had his grip as Mickey croaked, "Salt."

It was a long minute before we broke Johnny's grip and not before several RA's came running over writing down names. Shep pulled them aside and told them it was all a joke. Johnny looked like he could re-explode at any second. Only Mickey was still laughing.

Johnny Puma had a girlfriend, Wanda the Witch. Nobody liked Wanda, except Johnny. If Johnny knew everything, Wanda thought she did. She had an opinion on everything. She knew football, she knew basketball, she knew boxing and after Johnny got her to jog a mile around the track without stopping, she knew running too.

Mickey's connection to Wanda was biology. The piece meal investigation of reproduction, the organs and steps to birth can leave one confused with little clue how the pieces fit together. But Wanda the Witch knew it all.

Human reproduction for a Catholic girl from Philly was something that happened to someone else. Most were educated in same sex schools. What the girls knew about the boys was limited to sweat and the "thing."

Except for Wanda. Wanda asked the tough questions. She used the "p" word in mixed company. She knew that all semen were not in the navy. But it was her need to show all she knew that loaded Mickey's gun.

"I understand," Wanda began, "if the ejaculate," the professor had not used that word. Wanda liked big words. Looks were exchanged in class. Ejaculate. "...if the ejaculate is scientifically determined to be 85% carbohydrate," she asked earnestly, "if carbohydrate is a sugar, why does semen taste so salty?"

Taste salty. It took Mickey a second. He all but stood and cheered. Lunch could not come soon enough. The class erupted in laughter. Wanda turned to explain. It was too late. Nobody heard a word.

Mickey got to the table and sat. He waited for the table to get full. He began his story matter-of-fact. "You'll never guess what happened in Bio today..." and he told about a girl who asked a really dumb question. What a laugh he got. Everyone laughed. Johnny laughed.

Johnny laughed until Mickey said, "Wanda said it." That stopped everything.

For a short second there was a confused silence, and then all hell broke loose. Johnny moved with great intent. Johnny made his lunge over the table and caught Mickey by the neck. The table lifted and everything else went flying. Mickey laughed like a devil.

With his grip broken Johnny sank into his chair. He sat emotionless. Mickey gathered his tray. There were fingerprints on his neck. Mickey rose to leave.

"Johnny," Mickey was calm, "no hard feelings," he turned to leave, stopped and turned back, "I only got one question." Johnny sat like a stone. "Johnny, does Wanda have the whitest teeth you've ever come across?" and he ran laughing for his life.

Johnny had no response. I think everybody thought Mickey's last shot was pretty funny but nobody was laughing. Nobody dared. A minute or two later Johnny got up and left. He did not say good-bye.

Randy ROTC had no clue what happened. He looked at Eddie John Denny and said, "I don't get it. How would Wanda know semen was salty unless..."

Eddie John Denny held up his hand to cut Randy ROTC off, "Later, I'll tell you later."

THE BET

Johnny Puma was on the edge. For such a good week Johnny was having a terrible week. You would think that getting named to the "4 by 1" at Penn would have had him walking on air. It was only another brick on the load.

Johnny had a great indoors running 4:08. He ran that time twice outdoors and was training like a horse. He was fit and healthy and ready for a 4:06, on a bad day. But something worried Johnny more than a bad day.

This was Johnny's big chance. His college career was always a day late and a dollar short. He knew this would be his only chance for a Penn watch. Probably more important if he did not come through, Duke would not get the Penn Relays watch record. Being part of that failure would be like a bad tattoo.

Mickey had made himself scarce after the Wanda disclosure. Johnny was still licking his wounds. He ate alone. All his screws were getting a little tight. Nobody pressed him.

But Frank came to lunch on cloud nine. His feet were barely touching the ground. He had begged Coach Frier to let him run the marathon at Penn. He had never run that far but he though he could do it. After several weekend 20 milers and an easy one-twenty half he felt confident he could cruise home in 2:45

or so without much trouble. He had no aspirations to win, just get one under his belt.

Randy ROTC quizzed Frank about his shoes. "You know Abebe Bakila won the Rome Olympics in his bare feet!"

Frank deftly fielded the absurdity of Randy's question by telling him that he had a new pair of penny loafers he would break in on the run.

Returning to reality Frank said he hoped to hit 20 miles in about two hours and coast the rest of the way home. Randy slid his slide rule trying to give Frank accurate per mile splits when Johnny boomed from the next table, "You never cruise home! You always run to win! You gotta run to win."

There was a pause and then Johnny added in a guttural tone, "You'll never even finish. You have no right running that race."

Wow! That set everyone back on their heels, even though we were sitting. It was an ugly moment. I felt it in my stomach. I said to myself, "Here we go again." I did not feel as bad for Frank as I did for Johnny. He was unraveling before our eyes.

Frank was stunned to silence. Charlie Checkers got mad and immediately fired back, "You have no right to say that." And in spite of our differences Charlie was right.

"Maybe you better just worry about finishing yourself." Frank pointed at Johnny. Hearts beat loud in the silence. "Here we go again, here we go again," I repeated to myself. I looked for Johnny to strike. This was not good. No one was moving towards neutral ground.

Shep sat the detached observer throughout the exchanges. Things were always competitive but this was not competitive. This was not "the team."

"I think Frank will probably," probably was drawn out with special emphasis, "probably finish," he said looking at Johnny while pointing his fork at Frank, "but there is no way he'll break three hours," and he gave a little shrug to the Rover Boys.

Shep bent the confrontation in another direction. All the protests by Frank and Charlie and Mickey were simply answered by Shep with a, "No."

Charlie got particularly excited, pointing across the table to Shep, "I'll bet you 20 bucks Frank breaks three." In an instant money became the issue.

That set off a few rounds of "You're full of it," which elevated the mood slightly, but significantly. Shep was not betting, yet. I thought Frank could break three pretty easy, that seemed to be the hinge. Mickey slapped the table, "I'll bet $10 a minute Frank breaks three!" Now, the money was getting serious.

For a good 10 minutes there was a lot of snapping on who could do what. Shep and Mickey countered several times before settling on $1 per minute for every minute under three, $2 per minute for every minute over.

Randy ROTC was handling the higher math, "If Frank runs 2:45 he wins $15!" he blurted, like it was King Tut's fortune.

Shep was on a roll, so he pressed, "I want 50 bucks for a 'no start'."

Frank countered for the record, "I'll be there!"

Johnny, all but forgotten, but still simmering at the next table was quick to add, "And 50 bucks for a DNF!"

"I'll be there!" was all Frank had to say, his glare said the rest.

Shep tore a page out of Rhino's notebook and wrote everything down. He made everybody sign it. It was no guts, no glory, either you put up or shut up.

And then Shep tore another page out of Rhino's notebook. Rhino's eyes got wide, but Shep never saw it. "I'm doing a 50/50 raffle, predict Frank's race time." He passed the sheet around the table with, "A dollar up, a dollar in." The sheet stopped at Randy.

Randy would not touch the sheet. "Gambling is illegal in the NCAA."

Shep reached for the sheet, "Fuck the NCAA."

Randy's hand slapped the page in place. "If this is a 50/50 raffle, where does the other 50 go?"

Shep did not miss a beat, "My favorite charity." That got a big laugh at the table, and then Randy signed his name at 2:47:24. He told us the :24 was for good luck.

Shep grabbed the page, stood and addressed the lunch room, "50/50 raffle, pick a time for the Penn Relays Marathon!" You can not be convincing unless you are enthusiastic and Shep was brimming.

Randy sat in awe and spoke to no one in particular, "If it is a 50/50 raffle, who does the other 50 go to?" he emphasized the who.

I watched Shep work the room. He moved from table to table, nodding, pointing, carrying a fist full of dollars like a guy at a gas station. In a silence you could hear, "The one in the middle, that's Frank..." and "2:15...sure that's a good guess. Hey, you never know, it might be windy."

Shep made Frank a star and secretly stole a brick from Johnny. And the pedestrians donated their money to a guy who had more angles than a con man, which once I realized what he had done, I had to smile, because he was all of that, and more.

45.2

Randy ROTC was a sharp man with stats. He knew every world, American, collegiate and high school record, in every event. Sometimes you doubted what he said but he was always right.

"You know," he spoke to no one in particular, "I bet no one knows who the first man to run four minutes was?"

Those that did not say Roger Bannister were ignoring Randy.

"Nope," he beamed, "It was Derek Ibbotson from England. He ran 4:00.0 in a race where Herb Elliot ran 3:55.4."

Nobody liked a trick question. Randy had a copy of Jim Dunaway's *The Four Minute Mile* and was now a font of mile trivia.

"You know," changing the subject, "when Larry James and Lee Evans broke 44 in the 400 at Mexico City it was the first time two men broke 44 in the same race."

It was a so-what fact. Everybody knew that. Runners rate themselves and each other by quarters and miles. Everybody knows everybody else's quarter time and mile times. Randy was on a ramble.

"I saw," Jay Brown emphasized the 'saw,' "I saw Larry James be the first man to break 44 at Penn." This was Jay's favorite story. "I was a freshman. All I remember was the whooo..." He made a noise like a ghost train. "It sounded just like that."

I had heard parts of Jay's story before. It was a relief to hear someone else talk. Everyone felt the same. Jay had our attention.

"Larry got the stick about 15 yards behind this white guy from Duke or Army," he scanned the table. With everyone listening he became more animated. "I forget where the guy was from but Larry was cooking around the first turn, but he didn't make up a step."

The back legs of his chair scraped against the floor as he rose from his seat. "Larry comes off the turn and put the hammer down." Now Jay is pumping his arms, "He tunes up this guy in about five steps and it's ...later!" He broke into a big smile, did the whooo sound again and sat down.

"And you know what the funny thing is?" he had us all hanging on his question, "Guess what time the guy ran that got tuned up?"

Eddie John Denny was silent and quiet. He looked Jay right in the face and said, "I know, the guy ran 45.2." Eddie John Denny spoke with a certain certainty. "Save for the 43.9 it was the fastest split of the day. The guy ran for Army, West Point, not Duke and his name was Schrader, Hank Schrader." His tone was "no big deal."

Jay's jaw dropped. If Eddie John Denny had slapped him in the face he would not have been more surprised. Eddie John Denny stole the story right out from under him.

"I went to Bobby Knight's basketball camp, the guy at Indiana, he used to coach West Point." It was all matter-of-fact to Eddie John Denny. "He took us over to the track to watch Hank run. He said he wanted us to see a champion." Eddie John Denny just shrugged.

And then he added, "Coach Knight caught me sitting on a basketball, so he sat on MY head!" Eddie John Denny gave a detached laugh. That is a thrill only a rare person would pay for. Eddie John Denny returned to reality with, "Yeah, I know Hank."

"45.2," mused Randy ROTC, "I'd take that on a bad day."

We all stared at Randy but Shep spoke first, "Hey Randy, what is the record for keeping your trap shut?"

There was a long silence, but it was not long enough.

EPIPHANY AT THE PIE SHOPPE

James Joyce used a literary device called the epiphany. It is where a character has a sudden insight or realization and in a moment is transformed from innocence to experience.

There is the story about the two guys out hiking in the woods when they see a bear. One guys stops to put on his spare track shoes. The other guy says, "What are you doing? You know we can't out run a bear!" To which the first guy answers, "I don't have to out run the bear!" Number two, also called "the lunch" has just had an epiphany.

The Pie Shoppe at Villanova was what other colleges would call the student center. They did not sell pies but you could get a cheese steak, a milk shake or several other delicacies that promoted heart disease and tooth decay.

The NCAA used to allow colleges to legally give money to athletes on a monthly basis called "laundry money." This $15. could be used for whatever the athlete desired. At Villanova all varsity athletes were given $15 in Pie Shoppe tickets; 10 orange movie tickets worth $1.50 each, redeemable at the Pie Shoppe for cheese steaks, milk shakes or whatever you wanted.

The Irish guys had it rough from time to time. The pressure to produce was tremendous — personal, team, from a nation. They were tough competitors who shared a common bond that formed a strong support group in the tough times.

Ian lived a few doors down from me. Every so often he would stop by my room at about 9:30 p.m. and say, "I'll buy if you'll fly," meaning he would pay for whatever at the Pie Shoppe if I would go get it. He would reel off five or six orange movie tickets and 10 minutes later I would return with two cheese steaks, two milk shakes and some cookies. I made so many trips to the Pie Shoppe I got to know the cashier on a first name basis. She was a nice old lady.

Things were winding down for the spring term. Ian took me into his room to "show me something." He dug deep into his closet and pulled a six inch roll of orange movie tickets from the back of the closet. I was stunned. Where did he get all the tickets? This was corruption. Who in the athletic department was responsible for this?

On a vow of secrecy he told me the truth. This was a secret only the Irish guys knew. He pulled off a ticket and told me to look at it. I still could not figure out who had given him all the tickets.

I looked at the ticket. The only thing I saw was some numbers and an "Admit One,"

"No look," he said, "see...they are printed in Philadelphia!"

I still did not get it. "We looked up the print shop in the phone book and everyone bought their own roll of tickets for about ten bucks!" Ian said with great excitement.

There had to be at least 1,000 tickets on a roll. Not a bad investment for ten bucks.

"That's a lot of cheese steaks!" I laughed with excitement. This was a jackpot! I thought how absolutely clever this had all been done and that no one on the team had a clue what was going on.

But then I realized this could be a big offense. They could trace the numbers. One thousand tickets is a lot of cheese steaks. I asked him what he was going to do if he got caught.

He gave me a stunned look, "What do you mean if I get caught? You are the one that has been using them for the last six months!" And then he laughed an innocent laugh.

My epiphany. Oh, did I suffer the rest of the term. I would not have gone near the Pie Shoppe if they were giving free, I mean really free, cheese steaks or milk shakes.

Just before the term ended word spread that there would be no more "Pie Shoppes" next year. Coach Frier told Shep at the table that there had been "problems" with the system. After Frier left I looked at Shep and said, "No more free lunch."

Duke must have caught the smile in my voice. He gave me an almost startled look. I gave him a knowing nod and went back to my lunch.

THE SPED ARROW

I raised my hand with hesitation. Volunteering to answer one of Fr. Papin's questions could be a risky proposition. Of late things had gone well. Fr. Papin had chosen me to be in his research group. He picked the top five students in the class and me. I do not know why he chose me. I did not ask.

I looked at Fr. Papin and spoke calmly, "There are only three things that cannot be recalled, the sped arrow, the spoken word and the missed opportunity." It was a quote my father had told me countless times. Fr. Papin stared right at me.

Fr. Papin's stare could make a statue nervous. I felt the need to elaborate, "That was a saying by a Greek named Xenophon." I had only found that out by accident the week before. "Xenophon was a Greek," I repeated.

"I know that," said Fr. Papin. Of course he knew that. I felt stupid in a second. "That was an excellent point," Fr. Papin addressed the class and with a sweeping gesture of his hand, "You should applaud him."

And they did. He had never done this before. My stock was rising. About a week later I took another chance and said something else that generated applause. My stock jumped.

Part of my Papin penance was a paper on education. It was seven pages long. I worked hard. The semester came to an end. He never gave me my mark. I guess it was okay.

On the final day of class Fr. Papin asked me to run an errand for him. I was to deliver some papers to his three o'clock class. It was no problem. I was glad to do it.

I arrived at his class during attendance. I stood in silence as he methodically called off the alphabet. Everyone was there.

At the end of the roll Fr. Papin motioned me to his desk. I delivered his papers. He said, "Thank you" and asked me to introduce myself to the class. My rehabilitation had evidently progressed to his satisfaction. I scanned the class. There were a few familiar faces, not many, but some.

I gave my name and prepared to leave when Fr. Papin asked, "Please tell the class what you have learned from me this year."

I paused a long moment. There were so many things. Truth, the paper, hard work, personal improvement — where could I start?

If he had asked me how I had matured I could have reeled off three quick things, maybe five. What did I learn from him? What did I learn from Fr. Papin?

It came to me in a flash. I smiled, "Fr. Papin," I spoke with a certain confidence. I felt I knew Fr. Papin. All the work I had done, we had a good relationship. We were buddies. With a big smile I looked at him and said, "Fr. Papin, the most important thing I learned from you this year is that I never want to take another course from you!"

I turned to his class and waited for the laughter that never came. I looked back to Fr. Papin and had that back to Brooklyn feeling all over again.

He raised his hand, but not his voice and pointed to the door. "You have learned nothing. Get out."

In truth, I believe that was the only time Fr. Papin was ever wrong. I turned and in four short steps I was through the door. I never saw him again. I never got the chance to say "thanks."

THE RED BALLOON

Ian toed the line like he had done a million times before. The hand that held the dart was connected to the wrist that wore the new Penn Relays watch. He raised his dart to eye level and fired ...bull's eye! It made little difference to him or anyone else that he was aiming for the 20. Ian raised both arms and gave a yelp for joy. Everyone else cheered also. It was a magical end to a magical day.

I sat away from the game. Ian looked at me and pointed. The gold on his watch glistened. I smiled and pointed back. He had his first win at Penn only hours before and his feet had not touched the ground yet.

Randy ROTC, interpreter of the obvious, announced, "You got a bull's eye!" and for a silent second everyone looked at Randy. Nothing was going to spoil this evening.

Kelly's was the Villanova bar. In a land of 21 drinking Kelly's found a way of accommodating all patrons. The bar was dark, the juke box was loud and the team was all there. There were never many women at Kelly's. You went to Kelly's to drink. You went elsewhere for the women.

Shep stood apart and quiet. He had anchored the two mile relay and ran a leg on the DMR. It was his last Penn Relays. These two wins made five. He was unusually pensive. His time had come and gone. I imagined him mulling over the memories. He had reached a plateau few ever ascend to. Maybe there were no words for his thoughts. He directed his subway stare at Ian and a sad smile came to his eyes.

And in walked the Rover Boys — Charlie, Frank and Eddie John Denny, loud and sun burned to a crisp. They were red as a lobster from an afternoon on the top deck of Franklin Field. Frank held his hands in a guard position, "You can laugh," he said, slowly turning, "but just don't touch!"

Eddie John Denny was on the loose. He wore a pair of white shoes, pale blue slacks and a polyester shirt opened three buttons down. In his right hand he held three balloons — red, white and blue.

Shep came to life, "Disco! Where you goin'?"

Everyone laughed. Eddie John Denny placed his left hand on his stomach and let the balloons slowly raise his right hand. His white shoes did a little mock shuffle right and left.

"I got a date!" was drowned out with "oooh's."

"I got a date with a hooper from Immaculatta!"

"Does she spit?" Shep was alive. The Immaculatta team was the best women's team in the nation. They played like guys, and some spit too! Girls in high tops, it was a trip.

"I hope..." Eddie John Denny slid right, "...to find out..." then sled left, "...if she'll duck, spit or swallow!" and he spun around in a circle just like the Jackson Five. We went crazy.

Frank stood next to the bar shaking his head. He had a "marathon hangover" and confessed he was a hurting pup. He told me they had split a quick six back at the dorm. Frank had run 2:42 and change at the Penn Marathon. He put $10. of Johnny Puma's money on the bar and ordered a round of drinks. On the count of three they were gone.

On the count of five they were full again, and gone. Frank shook his head and breathed fire. Charlie slapped his hand on the bar. Eddie John Denny kicked his heel on the floor and did another 360° spin. I stacked the shot glasses in a little pyramid.

The Rover Boys readied to leave. "The picture, the picture," I grabbed for the picture, "Sign the picture!" I thrust the picture of St. David's Church that Kelly's put out each year. The bar was loaded with copies of the same initialed picture, back into the 50's.

Eddie John Denny carefully etched, "EJD was here!" and he added a Don Martin smile. Frank signed off. Charlie was in a hurry to go.

It was almost nine. Frank asked me if I wanted to join them. I looked at Jackson, he just shook his head. If the Man from Japan could not score, no one could. Mickey took my slot. My game of darts was soon up anyway. Amid cheers, balloons and well wishes the Rover Boys left the bar.

I turned in my seat and looked at the picture. My beer was kicking in. Names, all the names, who would ever see this? Who would ever care? I was...

The crash was ungodly. The whole building shook. I staggered from my stool. The shot glasses scattered on the bar. People groped for the walls, or floor. There was a silence and the pinball rang "tilt." The silence was forever.

I steadied my legs. The clock said 9 p.m.. I thought of the poem by TS Eliot. I was sobering quickly. The silence expanded.

Shep opened the door and was bathed in light. He squinted and raised his arm to shield his eyes. An engine was running, chugging to right itself. It chugged and gently rocked the vehicle. It was a truck.

Inside the truck was Tony the Parrot. His eyes were wild with disbelief. His head reared back and blood oozed from his mouth. He raised his arm but his wrist hung limp. His chin and neck were covered with blood.

I stood behind Shep on the steps, blinded by the light. Jack pushed his way through. He yelled for someone to call the police and an ambulance. He shut off the engine and lights of Tony the Parrot's truck. I looked at the ground. There was pizza and pizza boxes everywhere.

Mickey was the first to scream. We moved to him in slow motion. The windshield of the car was gone. Mickey screamed at the top of his lungs. He could not have screamed any louder. Mickey's nose was smashed and running blood, but it was his leg that caused the pain. The bone from his thigh, white and jagged pierced his jeans. There was blood everywhere. I went to swallow and vomited. I was sober.

Jack was moving quickly. "Do you smell gas?" I did not but sniffed anyway. The air was hot. It was a hot humid night but there was no gas.

Charlie stirred in the back seat. The door on his side of the car was ripped away. Mechanically he crawled through the open space. He used the car for support but it did not help. He took two short steps and collapsed. His head made a hollow sound when it hit the street. He began to wrench.

Frank was gone. His door was wide open, but he was gone. I scanned the street. People in other cars stopped and came running. A crowd was gathering. In the distance was a faint siren. Where was Frank?

I heard my name. It was Ian, on the sidewalk, near a tree. He called me again. I counted my steps towards Ian. I saw a shoe, a white shoe and then the leg of a body and blood, more blood than I had ever seen.

At Ian's feet lay Eddie John Denny, his heart beating his life away. I stood transfixed. There was nothing we could do. Blood oozed from his ear. I knelt and blessed myself. Jesus, Jesus, Jesus, no one was ever supposed to die. The red balloon dragged its ribbon along the ground, then popped.

THE EMPTY TABLE

The mood at the table was black. Everyone was up all night. The students knew something had happened to the runners. They turned and looked and wondered in mumbled voices.

The chance to moralize was great, but no one did. Alcohol, driving, stupidity, who knew? It was not going to change anything. The dye was cast.

Charlie and Eddie John Denny were the first to leave. They sped away in an ambulance. There were red lights flashing everywhere and sirens and blips. The street was chaos.

Mickey screamed all the while he was in the car. When they cut the roof off he got quiet. He was bleeding to death. When he got quiet we thought he was going to die too.

Coach Frier stopped by the table to say that Jumbo was taking care of things. There was a long pause. No one really knew what "things" were. No one asked.

Johnny Puma had gotten in to see Mickey. He said he was pretty groggy and couldn't say much. Mickey's leg was all bandaged and hung up on pulleys. Eddie John Denny clung to life critical but stable.

Frank was under observation. Officer Rizzo, The Weasel, had found him about 2 a.m. walking around the track. The Weasel stopped by the table.

"I found your boy walking around the track," he volunteered the information like he deserved a medal. "He was wearing one shoe and told me he was looking for the finish line!" The Weasel thought that was funny. Nothing could be funny this day. We sat stone faced. The Weasel was a creep.

"Officer Rizzo," Randy ROTC began in all earnestness, "Officer Rizzo, could I share something with you?"

Randy spoke with his usual formal tone. He stared The Weasel right in the eye. Randy never gave The Weasel a chance to answer, "Officer Rizzo I feel safe saying that you always have been, and are, and will always be an asshole."

Randy's tone remained matter of fact but it drew more than a few stares. Shep shook his head and smiled. Randy never took his eyes off The Weasel who wrinkled his nose, mumbled a curse and headed for the door.

Randy's gaze never let The Weasel go until he disappeared through the door. Randy was amazing, maybe there was hope for the boy yet.

Then we settled back into our silence, distractedly picking at cold eggs and dry toast. What could anyone say? What could anyone do?

Duke tapped his fork on his plate, raised his head and announced, "I'm doing the Frolic," and rose from the table.

Somebody else volunteered the Radnor and there was an "…anything but the Big Hill." The chairs scraped the floor. We picked up our trays and left the table empty.

EPILOGUES

KEYS TO THE KINGDOM

Sometimes I used to sit at the table and wonder. I would look around and wonder who was going to make it. Who it was going to be. Somebody was going to make it. You had your hopes.

And we all had our dreams. We all entered pretenders to the crown. We left accountants, teachers, engineers. The time went fast, but never fast enough. It was always about Time. Our lives were dedicated and spent in getting more in less. We chased a vanishing point.

College ended and jobs, marriage, families — life lead in all directions. You see old friends at track meets, weddings or by chance on a subway, a restaurant, a vacation. There is always a story. You play catch-up for a few moments, say good-bye, maybe never to meet again.

Years later I sat alone in the Garden. Ian stood among the white flashes at the finish line of the Wanamaker Mile. He had won his third mile victory. He had joined a select few. The fact that there would be world records and more Wanamaker Miles to come could not have sweetened the moment.

With steady arms he raised the silver plaque above his head, his defining moment. We all had our chance. We all had our fun. Some men dream dreams, other men see visions. I felt proud that one of us had beaten the lock.

JAKE, HEAVEN

They had a thing at Villanova that all the buildings on campus had to be named for a priest. It was one of those traditions that had evolved that the administration chose to follow. The old Field House was built in the 30's. Everything about it was small. The rumor had it that the money for the gym was donated by Al Capone. There were no dedication plaques in the building.

The DuPonts own Delaware. I am not sure what the connection to Villanova was but the family contacted the school in the early 70's with a plan to build a new field house, The DuPont Center. The school said they would take the money but could not break the priest tradition. No new field house was built.

Fast forward to 1985. Villanova makes the NCAA basketball final. It is an unlikely group. The team had modest success in the rigorous Big East. The team ascended through the NCAA Tournament with lucky shots and little more. Cinderella had made it to the ball.

The NCAA Championship game was Georgetown-Villanova. John Thompson had assembled a supporting cast around Patrick Ewing that was unbeatable. Georgetown's victories to the Final Four were methodical and matter-of-fact. In the two regular season games Villanova had lost. It was never supposed to be a game. It was never a "game."

You could not say what happened was a tactic. Georgetown out shot Villanova 54 to 28. The only thing that kept Villanova in the game was that they did not miss. Every pass that set up every point was destined for the bottom of the net.

Throughout the game the television camera panned to the Villanova bench. Crippled and wheelchair bound Jake sat at the end. He was dying of Lou Gerhig's Disease. To the unknowing Jake was an object of pity. Those that knew Jake, knew better. In front of 20 million people he spent the night dipping his hand into his bucket of Lucky Charms helping the Villanova team do something they could not.

Some might dismiss this as the last selfish wish of a dying old man, but I prefer to believe it was God's gift to a man who had spent a lifetime taping ankles. There was more going on that night than just basketball. Villanova shot 79% from the floor. Georgetown was history.

The DuPont's finally bought and built the DuPont Center. All the other buildings on campus are still named for priests: Austins, Sheehans, Sullivans, except one — The Jake Nevin Field House. They named that one for a saint.

Russ Ebbets

Author

Dr. Russ Ebbets is on the faculty at New York Chiropractic College in Seneca Falls, NY. In addition to a successful athletic career Dr. Ebbets coached at the high school and college levels. A popular clinician, Dr. Ebbets studied athletic development in the former Soviet Union and has worked with USA Track and Field's Coaching Education Program since 1985. His training tips and running editorials have appeared in numerous running magazines and journals. *SUPERNOVA* is his first novel.

Joe McDowell

Cover Artist

Joe McDowell taught art and coached cross country/track and field at Nyack High School in New York's Rockland County for 31 years. During his tenure as coach his teams won eight Section IX Team Championships. His program produced four individuals NYS Champions, one Eastern States Champion and two representatives to the "Golden West." Upon "retirement" Coach McDowell spent seven years as the assistant coach at Hartwick College. In May 1995, Joe McDowell was elected to the Rockland County Sports Hall of Fame.

ORDER FORM

☎ Telephone orders: Call Toll Free: 1-800-879-4214. Have your VISA or MasterCard ready.

✉ Postal Orders: Bookcrafters Order Dept., 615 E. Industrial Dr., Chelsea, MI 48118 USA

📄 Bulk or Team Orders: Call 1-800-484-1205, ext. 9375

Please send _____ copies of **SUPERNOVA** @ $10.95

Name: _____
Address: _____
City: _____ State _____ Zip: _____
Telephone: (_____) _____

Sales Tax:
Please add 7.0% for books shipped to New York addresses.
Shipping:
Book Rate: $1.50 for the first book and 75 cents for each additional book. (Ground shipping may take 3 - 4 weeks)
Air Mail: $3.50 per book
Payment:
❑ Check   ❑ Money Order

Call *toll free* and order now

ORDER FORM

☎ Telephone orders: Call Toll Free: 1-800-879-4214. Have your VISA or MasterCard ready.

✉ Postal Orders: Bookcrafters Order Dept., 615 E. Industrial Dr., Chelsea, MI 48118 USA

📄 Bulk or Team Orders: Call 1-800-484-1205, ext. 9375

Please send _____ copies of **SUPERNOVA** @ $10.95

Name: _____
Address: _____
City: _____ State _____ Zip: _____
Telephone: (_____) _____

Sales Tax:
Please add 7.0% for books shipped to New York addresses.
Shipping:
Book Rate: $1.50 for the first book and 75 cents for each additional book. (Ground shipping may take 3 - 4 weeks)
Air Mail: $3.50 per book
Payment:
❑ Check   ❑ Money Order

Call *toll free* and order now

ORDER FORM

☎ Telephone orders: Call Toll Free: 1-800-879-4214. Have your VISA or MasterCard ready.

🖅 Postal Orders: Bookcrafters Order Dept., 615 E. Industrial Dr., Chelsea, MI 48118 USA

📰 Bulk or Team Orders: Call 1-800-484-1205, ext. 9375

Please send _____ copies of **SUPERNOVA** @ $10.95

Name: _____
Address: _____
City: _____ State _____ Zip: _____
Telephone: (_____) _____

Sales Tax:
Please add 7.0% for books shipped to New York addresses.
Shipping:
Book Rate: $1.50 for the first book and 75 cents for each additional book. (Ground shipping may take 3 - 4 weeks)
Air Mail: $3.50 per book
Payment:
❑ Check   ❑ Money Order

Call *toll free* and order now